One More Chance

One More Chance

A Rosemary Beach Novel

Abbi Glines

ATRIA PAPERBACK

New York • London • Toronto • Sydney • New Delhi

ATRIA PAPERBACK

A Division of Simon & Schuster, Inc.
1230 Avenue of the Americas
New York, NY 10020

First Atria Paperback edition September 2014

ATRIA PAPERBACK and colophon are trademarks of Simon & Schuster, Inc.

For information about special discounts for bulk purchases, please contact Simon & Schuster Special Sales at 1-866-506-1949 or business@simonandschuster.com.

The Simon & Schuster Speakers Bureau can bring authors to your live event. For more information or to book an event, contact the Simon & Schuster Speakers Bureau at 1-866-248-3049 or visit our website at www.simonspeakers.com.

Interior design by Dana Sloan
Cover photo © iStockPhoto

Manufactured in the United States of America

10 9 8 7 6 5 4 3 2 1

Library of Congress Cataloging-in-Publication Data is available.

ISBN 978-1-4767-5657-8
ISBN 978-1-4767-5659-2 (ebook)

To my brother, Jody Potts. You inspired this part of Grant and Harlow's journey with a love story from your past. I've never forgotten it, and now I know why it stuck with me all these years.

"That moment when you realize you've completely fucked up your life . . . yeah, I know that moment. All too well."

—GRANT CARTER

Grant

"It's me, but then you know that. This is the forty-eighth message . . . which means I haven't seen your face in forty-eight days. I haven't held you. I haven't seen your smile. I don't know where you are, Harlow. I've looked, baby. God, I've done everything I could. Where are you? Are you even listening to these messages? Your voice-mail box is all I have left of you. I fucked up. I fucked up so bad. Just call me or answer my calls or send me a text. No, call me. Don't just text me. I need to hear your voice. I just . . . I need to see you, Harlow. I can't make this right if I can't hold you—"

BEEP

Another message cut off. Damn voice mail never let me finish. But then I wasn't sure she was even listening to her voice mail. I'd been calling every damn night since the moment she walked out my door, and still nothing. I had gone to her dad's house in Los Angeles, and no one had been there, though I hadn't been able to see for myself—I wasn't even allowed past the gate. Security threatened to call the police.

Rush assured me she wasn't in Beverly Hills. But he knew where she was. She had told him where she was going the day she left my house for the last time, but he wouldn't tell me. He said she needed time, and I had to give it to her. The night he told me he couldn't tell me where she was, I had planted my fist in his face for the first time since we'd known each other. He'd taken the hit and shaken it off like the badass he was. Then he'd warned me that was my only shot. He understood, but the next time, he would be fighting back.

I had felt like a shithead for hitting him. He was protecting Harlow, and she needed someone to protect her. I just couldn't stand not being able to hold her. Not explaining why I had acted like a jackass.

Blaire had just started talking to me again. She'd been so mad at me when she'd seen the bruise on Rush's face and his bloody nose. She'd refused to speak to me for almost a month.

I couldn't talk to anyone but Harlow's voice mail.

I would wake up in the morning and go to work doing manual labor for one of my construction jobs. I needed the physical abuse in order to sleep at night. Once the sun set and I couldn't work anymore, I would come home, eat, take a bath, call Harlow's voice mail, and go to bed. Then I would do it all over again the next day.

Nannette had stopped trying to contact me. After I kept refusing to answer her calls or the door when she came over, she got the hint and left me alone. Seeing her only brought back all the pain I'd caused Harlow, and I hated seeing Nan's face. I didn't need any more reminders of all I had done to hurt Harlow.

Was it possible to hate yourself? Because I was pretty damn sure I did. Why hadn't I controlled the shit pouring out of my mouth the last time I'd seen Harlow? I'd ruined it. I'd hurt her. Remembering her face as I'd ranted about her not telling me about her illness made it impossible for me to look in the mirror. She had been scared, and I had been worried about me and my fucking fears. How had I become so selfish? I had been terrified of losing her, but all I'd done was send her running.

I was a bastard, a heartless bastard. I didn't deserve her, but I wanted her more than I wanted to breathe.

I was losing precious time with her. I wanted to make sure she was safe and protected. I wanted to be there to take care of her and make sure she was healthy. Make sure her heart was OK. I didn't trust anyone else to keep her alive. *Fuck!* The idea of her being anything other than alive ripped open my chest, and I had to double over to breathe.

"You gotta call me, baby. I can't live like this. I have to be with you," I cried out into the empty room.

Harlow

Sitting on a hay bale with my knees pulled up under my chin and my arms wrapped around my legs, I watched my half brother, Mase, work with a young thoroughbred that was giving him fits. Having something to focus on other than my inner thoughts was easier. I found myself more worried about Mase breaking his neck than my own problems.

Tonight would come soon enough. My phone would ring, and then my voice mail would ding, alerting me that he had left another message. I would spend the next few hours staring at the wall while mixed emotions ran through me. I wanted to listen to Grant's voice mails. I missed him. I missed hearing his voice. I missed his dimpled smile. But I couldn't, even if he was sorry, and I had no doubt, after all the phone calls and his attempt to fight past the security at Dad's house, that he was sorry.

He was terrified of losing someone he cared about again. If I told him I was carrying our child inside me and that there was a possibility I wouldn't make it through the delivery, I was afraid he would want me to do what Mase wanted me to do. What the doctors suggested I do.

I loved Grant Carter. I loved him so much. But I loved

someone els
and placed
seen the s
any of th
already.
feel thi

I
won
My
tio
w
h
a
want.

The fear was there that
wouldn't make it. But I believed I wou
I wanted to love and hold my baby and show that
anything for it. I wanted a child of my own. I wanted it enough
to live. I was determined that I could do this. I would do this.

I wished Mase understood. I hated seeing the fear flash in
his eyes every time he glanced down at my stomach. He was
terrified because he loved me. I didn't want to scare him, but
he had to trust me. I could do this. From sheer willpower
alone, I could have this baby and live. As if Mase could hear
my thoughts, he jumped down off the horse and leveled his
gaze on me. Always the concern. I watched as he led the horse
back into the barn. We had been out here all morning, and
now it was lunchtime.

Mase's stepfather had given him some land at the back
of their property, and Mase had built a small log cabin on it.

Luckily for me, his thirteen-hund
two bedrooms. No one knew a
tucked out of sight, so when
mother's front door, she jus
and if they didn't get off
lice. Now that the me
harder to hide.
Since then, it
I had been ab
visit to the
been sta
told h
las

ed-square-foot home had

out this place, since it was

he media showed up at Mase's

told them neither of us was there,

the property, she would call the po-

dia knew me as Kiro's daughter, it was

had been silent. We didn't go into town, and

e to hide out in Mase's log cabin. Other than the

ob-gyn, which Mase's mother took me to, I had

ing in seclusion. Dad had called a few times. I hadn't

m about the pregnancy, but I had just found out myself

week.

Mase wanted to tell Kiro. He was sure Dad could force me to have an abortion. I knew it was pointless. I knew in my heart what I was going to do. No one was going to change that. And if my willpower to live wasn't enough, my baby would be loved. The one person standing by me in all of this had assured me that she would raise this child and love it as if it were her own. Maryann Colt was the mother every kid deserved. When I was little and would visit Mase, his mother would make us cookies and take us on picnics. She would tuck us in at night, and after she would kiss Mase's cheek and tell him she loved him, she would do the same to me. As if I belonged there.

And Maryann knew what it felt like to be a mother. She understood the need in me to protect this baby. She had held my hand when they confirmed that I was indeed pregnant. Her tears hadn't been of sorrow but of joy. She had been happy for me because I was happy. That evening was the first time I had ever heard Mase fight with his mother. Maryann had stood by me while I explained that I wasn't having an abortion. Mase had been furious. He'd ended up begging me to reconsider.

I knew that Grant would be worse. Telling myself that he had forgotten me or that he didn't care was pointless. I knew better. He still called me every day and left a message. He wanted forgiveness and was possibly ready to take that chance of loving someone with my condition. But now the risk was so much greater. In the end, I didn't think he would have enough strength to stick it out. I couldn't forget the words he'd said to me the last time I'd seen him. Our chance was over.

"You feeling OK?" Mase's voice interrupted my thoughts, and I covered my eyes from the sun and squinted up at him. He was dressed in his faded jeans and a blue plaid shirt. A fine layer of dust covered him from his morning activities, and the cowboy hat on his head was tilted back as he wiped the sweat on his forehead with a towel from his back pocket.

"I'm fine. Just lost in my thoughts," I explained.

He held out his hand to me. "Come on, let's go eat something. Momma will have lunch on the table by now." Maryann cooked a full meal for lunch every day. She said her guys needed it to keep going hard outside. Mase's stepfather was still using a walking stick after taking a tumble off his tractor, even though he'd already gotten his cast removed. Mase had been picking up his stepfather's slack for a while now, and he seemed relieved that he was back out working. His stepfather raised beef cattle, and his work was grueling. Mase was only used to training a few horses.

I slipped my hand into my brother's and let him pull me up. I wouldn't admit to him that I was weak from my loss of appetite. I wasn't nauseated from the pregnancy, but I missed

Grant. Right now, I wanted him. I wanted to share this with him. To see him smile and hear him laugh. I wanted more than he could give me.

"You haven't smiled in days," Mase said, letting go of my hand.

I dusted off my bottom and managed a shrug. "I'm not going to lie to you. I miss him. I love him, Mase. I admitted that to you already."

Mase fell into step beside me as we walked toward his parents' large white farm house with its wraparound porch and flowers in the window boxes. Mase had grown up with the perfect life. The kind that kids like me don't believe in unless they've seen it. I wanted to give that kind of life to my child.

"Answer his call tonight instead of sending it to voice mail. He wants to hear your voice. At least give him that. It might make you feel better," Mase said. This wasn't the first time he'd urged me to answer Grant's calls. I hadn't told Mase why I'd left. I couldn't stand the idea of Mase hating Grant. He wouldn't understand why Grant had reacted the way he had. And he'd never forgive him. They would be family one day. This baby would make them family.

And if I wasn't around . . .

"You're stubborn, Harlow Manning. You know that?" He nudged my shoulder with his arm.

"I'll answer him when it's time. It just isn't time yet."

Mase let out a frustrated sigh. "You're carrying his baby. He needs to know that. This ain't right, what you're doing."

I brushed the wisps of hair that had fallen out of my ponytail holder out of my face. He wouldn't understand why

I couldn't tell Grant. I was tired of having this conversation with him.

"No one will persuade me to give up my baby. I will not choose myself over this child. I can't. I won't. I just . . . don't ask me to again, just understand that I have to do this my way."

Mase tensed beside me. Any reminder that I was taking a gamble with my life upset him. But it was my life to choose. I didn't push him to agree. We walked in silence to the house.

Maryann stood over the stove in a blue and white polka-dotted apron, which I knew was monogrammed on the front. It had been a gift from me when I was seventeen. When the screen door slammed behind us, Maryann glanced over her shoulder and smiled. "Just about ready. Set the table for me, will you?" she said, then turned back to the stove.

Mase went to the silverware drawer, and I went for the plates. This had become a regular routine. After putting down four place settings, I went to get the mason jars and fill them with ice and sweet tea.

"Five places today. Major will be here for lunch. He called this morning to let me know he was on his way into town. Dad agreed to hire him for the next six months. He needs a break from the drama at home, and we need another strong pair of arms around here."

From what I remembered of Major, he was a bully. A scrawny, mean bully. But then, I hadn't seen Mase's cousin since he was ten, so things could have changed. He should be taller than four and a half feet and have his braces off by now.

"Uncle Chap still planning on divorcing this one?" Mase asked as concern wrinkled his brow. We never talked about his cousin, mostly because Major had lived in a different country

every time Mase had mentioned him. Uncle Chap was a Ma-
rine, and he was hard-core. He also made it his goal in life to
marry as many young, beautiful women as he could. Major
always had a new mom. That much I remembered.

Maryann sighed and set the biscuits on the table. "The
thing is, this time it isn't about some pretty young thing wanting a sugar daddy. Hillary also wanted Major, and apparently,
she got him. Major made a mistake, and, well, Chap isn't very
happy with his wife or his son. Major can't go home and face
his dad now, and he doesn't want to go back to college. He's
confused and unhappy."

Mase set the pitcher of tea on the table and swung a surprised
expression toward me. He hadn't known this bit of information.
Interesting. "You mean . . . Major tapped his stepmom?"

"Don't say *tapped*," Maryann said as she frowned at her son.
"And yes, he did. But Hillary was only four years older than
Major. What did Chap expect? He's an old man, and he married a young girl, then put her in a house with his beautiful
son while he went off to work all the time."

Mase let out a low whistle and then chuckled. "Major
tapped his stepmom," he said again.

"That's enough. He will be here any minute, and I know
he's embarrassed about all this. Be nice. Ask him about college or what he wants to do. Just don't talk about Hillary or
his dad."

I was trying hard not to look completely disturbed by
this. I couldn't picture Major as beautiful by any stretch of the
imagination. But then, all I knew was the ten-year-old Major,
not the twenty-one-year-old who could attract a woman who
shouldn't want him.

A swift knock on the door got our attention, and all eyes in the kitchen turned to the door as the grown-up version of Major Colt walked into the room.

His green eyes were almost emerald. I was surprised I hadn't remembered that. An unsure smile touched his face as he looked at his aunt and then at Mase. I took a quick glance at the rest of him. He had to be at least six-four now, and every inch of him was well built. Thick, corded arms that reminded me a lot of Mase's were showcased in the short sleeves of his gray T-shirt.

"So you slept with your stepmom." Those were the first words to break the silence. Of course, they came from Mase.

"Mase Colt-Manning, I am going to tan your hide," Maryann said in a stern voice, quickly wiping her hands on her apron and making her way to Major. The small smile that tugged at Major's lips as he looked at Mase made me think maybe he wasn't going to get as upset as Maryann thought he was. It wasn't like he was a kid who was taken advantage of. He was every bit a man.

He turned to look at Maryann but stopped when his eyes found me. He paused, then began grinning. A real smile this time. He recognized me. Not surprising, since my face had been all over the media the past two months.

"Well, if it ain't Little Miss Gone Missing," Major said. "You're even prettier than the photos they keep showing of you on TV."

"Easy," Mase said, and took a step to stand between Major and me. "I realize you're Casanova now, but she ain't available for romancing. I'm sure Uncle Chap will have a new wife soon, and you can see how long it takes to get in *her* pants."

"Enough!" Maryann said, slapping Mase on the arm like a naughty child before pulling Major into a hug. "We're thrilled you're here. Ignore your cousin's attempt at humor. He has no filter, and I apologize for that."

Major returned her hug and smirked at Mase over her head, which didn't even reach his shoulder. "Thanks, Aunt Maryann. I won't let him get to me. I can handle it, I swear."

"Unbelievable. He sleeps with his old man's wife, and you're taking up for him and babying him like he's the victim." Mase said, but there was no resentment in his tone. He was smiling as he said it.

The door opened again, and Mase's stepfather stepped inside. Even with a limp, he was still a looming presence. Height was definitely a Colt trait. "Glad you're here, boy," he said to Major. "But I'm hungry, so you're gonna have to let go of my wife so she can feed me."

Major laughed this time, a loud, full laugh that made us all smile.

Grant

"Message fifty-five. Each day, I think this will be the last day I get your voice mail. That you'll eventually answer me. I just want to hear your voice and know you're safe and happy. I want you happy. I'm fucking miserable. I'm losing sleep. You're all I think about. I miss you, baby. I miss you so bad. So damn bad. Just knowing you're safe and healthy would help. Rush assures me you're fine, but I need to hear it from you. Anything . . . I'll do anything. Just talk to me."

BEEP

I hated that sound. It mocked my pain and put an end to the few seconds when I felt like I had Harlow's ear. But she probably wasn't listening to my messages, anyway. I was pretty damn sure she would have called me by now if she had heard even one of my desperate voice mails. She wouldn't be able to ignore me.

Rush had told me she wasn't at Mase's mother's house in Texas, but I was about ready to visit Mase and find out what he knew. I didn't care about the extra security I'd been warned about. I would go to fucking jail if it meant I could get some answers. I would give anything to know where Harlow was.

My phone rang, and for a second, my heart stopped. For

a split second, I let myself hope it was Harlow. Even though, deep down, I knew it couldn't be her. Glancing down at the phone, I saw Rush's name lighting up the screen. He wasn't Harlow, but he was the only connection I had to her right now.

"What?" I said into the phone as I stared up at the ceiling.

"Not sure why I call your grumpy ass anymore," Rush replied.

I wasn't sure, either. But if he called, I would answer. Even if he didn't know where Harlow was, he was the only one I could bring myself to talk to about this. I felt he understood. He might be the only person who understood just how torn-up I was.

"It's late," I told him.

"It's not that late. Blaire just went upstairs to rock Nate to sleep."

Rush had his happy little life now. A wife he worshipped. A son he adored. I was happy he had everything he ever wanted. Neither one of us had known what a normal, healthy family was like. Now he did. Now he had that. But me . . . maybe I could have when Harlow was still here. Maybe.

"I know you're not in the mood to talk, but I'm just calling to check on you. Blaire mentioned that I needed to call you and see how you were before she went upstairs."

Apparently, Blaire really had forgiven me. I wished I could tell Rush I was fine. That I could breathe normally and my chest didn't continually ache. That I didn't feel lost and helpless. But I couldn't tell him that. The truth was, I needed Harlow.

"Were you OK when Blaire left you?" I asked him, knowing

the answer already. I had been there. I had forced him to get out of the house.

"No," he replied. "You know I was a complete mess."

"Yeah," was my only response. At that point, I hadn't understood him. But now it all made sense. He had been ripped in two, and he was expected to live each day like everything was normal, clinging to the hope she'd come back to him. "I'm sorry for making you leave your house and get out back then. I didn't get it."

Rush let out a low, hard chuckle. "It might have helped me some. Don't apologize. Sitting around thinking about it would have fucked me up worse. I didn't have a job to lose myself in every day like you do."

"Have you talked to her?" I asked, unable to help myself. I needed something. Anything.

"She's good. She's safe. She asked how you were. I told her you looked like shit and you weren't doing so great."

If she was listening to my voice mails, she would know that already. I wasn't holding anything back when I called her. I was wide open with her, baring my soul. "Will she ever forgive me?" I asked, closing my eyes, afraid of his answer.

"She already has. She just isn't ready to open up again yet. She's dealing with a lot right now. Her mother and Kiro, then this . . . just give her more time."

If she'd forgiven me, why wasn't she listening to my voice mails? Why wasn't she at least answering when I called? "Tell her I just want to hear her voice. She doesn't have to talk to me long—just a minute. I want to tell her I love her. I want to tell her I'm sorry. I . . . just need to tell her I need her."

Rush was silent a moment. Anyone else would have made fun of how vulnerable I had become. Not him. "I'll tell her. Get some sleep. Call me and check in some. Blaire worries."

I swallowed against the lump in my throat. We said our good-byes, and I dropped the phone to my chest and closed my eyes, letting images of Harlow fill my thoughts. They were all I had now.

Harlow

"Your phone's ringing," Mase said as he walked outside toward me with my phone in his outstretched hand. I was on the swing that had been hanging here in the yard since we were kids, alone with my thoughts.

"Who is it?" I asked, afraid to look. I was getting weak. If it was Grant, I wasn't sure I could ignore him anymore.

"Blaire," Mase replied, tossing the phone into my lap. "I'm heading down to the barn. Got some feed coming in, and I need to show Major what jobs I'm passing off to him now he's settled in. You need to talk to Blaire. Then think about calling Grant."

I touched Answer on my phone, then held it to my ear. "Hello?"

"Hey. Haven't heard from you in a few days. I wanted to check in and see how things were going." Blaire didn't know about the pregnancy. I trusted her with everything except keeping secrets from Rush. She'd tell him, and I knew Rush would tell Grant. He wouldn't be able not to. So I kept that secret close.

"I'm doing fine," I replied, not even believing my own voice. "How are things there?" I asked, unable to say his name.

"You mean, how's Grant? He isn't doing well. Still the same pattern. Lots of work and little sleep. He doesn't talk to anyone but Rush, and now he's begging Rush daily to tell him where to find you. He's pitiful, Harlow. He needs to hear your voice."

My heart squeezed, and I blinked away the tears in my eyes. Knowing he was hurting was hard to accept. But how could I call him and not break down on him and tell him how much I missed him? That wouldn't help anything. He would only be more hurt when I refused to tell him where I was. "I'm not ready," I told her.

Blaire let out a sigh, and I heard Nate's laughter in the background. Baby laughter was all I needed to remind myself why I couldn't let Grant know what was going on.

"Blaire, can I ask you something?" It was out of my mouth before I could stop myself.

"Of course," she replied.

Nate's little voice started chanting "Dada" over and over.

"Hold on a sec. Rush just walked in, and Nate gets excited when he sees his daddy. Let me take this in another room," Blaire said.

I wanted what Blaire had. More than anything . . . I wanted that. I wanted to watch Grant with our baby. The child we created. The child that was inside me. But would Grant want that?

"OK, I can hear you better now. What is it you want to ask me?"

Closing my eyes tightly, I hoped this wasn't a mistake. "Before Nate was born, would you have given your life for his? Did you love him that much?"

Blaire didn't answer. She was silent for several seconds, and

I started to think I'd said too much. That she would figure out why I was asking her this.

"He was a part of Rush and me. I would have done anything for him from the moment I knew he was inside me. So, yes," she said. Her words were slow and almost tortured, but I knew she was being honest. I also knew that she'd understand my choice. "But Rush wouldn't have felt the same way," she added.

The emotion clogging my throat made it difficult to respond. "Yeah. I didn't think so. I, uh, I need to go. I'll talk to you soon." I didn't wait for her to reply before ending the call, dropping my phone into my lap, and covering my face with both hands, letting the sorrow free. I sobbed for the life I might not be able to give my baby, for the possibility that I might not be there if the baby *was* born, and for the life I wanted so badly with Grant but feared I'd never have. I cried until all the tears dried up. Until I couldn't cry any more. Then I covered my stomach with my hands and sat there as the breeze dried my tear-streaked face. It was time I found the strength I needed to do this. To say I wasn't scared of dying was a lie. I was terrified, but I would do it if it meant this baby inside me could live. This life was a part of me and the man I loved. The only man I would ever love.

Before I'd met Grant, I hadn't known what it felt like to be completely in love. I had watched couples and daydreamed about the day a man would look at me with devotion and adoration in his eyes. I had imagined walking down the aisle toward a man who saw and loved only me. A man who loved me in all of my awkwardness. A man who loved me and my imperfect heart. For a moment, I was sure I had found that . . .

My thoughts were interrupted by Maryann's red Dodge truck coming down the gravel road that led from the white farmhouse to Mase's log cabin. Maryann hadn't been by in a couple of days. Major had been a good distraction for her. I knew my next doctor's appointment was coming up. They wanted me in every week since I was considered high-risk. But I wasn't sure which day she had set my next visit for.

Instead of going to lunch at the house, I had stayed here the past two days. Alone. I was safe alone. I also wanted to give them time to talk about family things with Major. I knew he wasn't comfortable discussing them in front of me. I wasn't his family. The only problem was, I had nothing to do to fill my time. I was left to my thoughts. Reading was something I used to escape into, but now I couldn't seem to stay focused on the story.

My thoughts were always on Grant and the future.

The truck came to a stop, Maryann's door swung open, and her jeans-clad legs swung out as she jumped down. She was a natural beauty. Every cowgirl I had ever imagined looked like Maryann to me. Tall and slender, always dressed in snug jeans, riding boots, and a button-down plaid shirt tied at her waist. The cowboy hat on her head was the finishing touch. It wasn't feminine at all but dirty and used.

She walked up the steps and turned to look at me with the concerned frown of a mother. A mother I'd never really had. "You trying to worry me, girl?" she asked, studying me closely.

I shook my head. "No, I'm sorry. I just haven't been hungry, and I need to be alone."

Her frown lines increased. "You been up here crying is what it looks like to me. Crying ain't good for you, your heart, or that baby. You gotta snap out of this. If you're crying over that Carter boy, then call him. Talk to him. You need the full force of your strength and willpower if you're gonna do this, girl. You can't be depressed and ready to give up."

I hadn't thought about that. But talking to Grant meant I could no longer protect him. "This will terrify him. I'm trying to keep him safe from this. His greatest fear in life is losing someone he loves."

Maryann put her hands on her hips and rolled her eyes. "You have got to be kidding me. Is that boy so much of a wimp that he can't handle life? If he's a real man, he'll step up and be the rock you need right now. If he can't do that, then he ain't worth your time."

She didn't know how broken Grant had looked when he'd found out about my heart. He was a wonderful man who had trusted me. I had kept something from him that would have spared him from getting hurt. If I had just told him about my heart the day he showed up in my room with Chinese food, he never would have risked this. He would have been safe. I wouldn't have known what it felt like to be held by him or touched, but he would be safe. His heart would be safe. I'd selfishly taken that choice away from him.

"He deserves more," I told her. That was all I could say.

"To hell he does. If he won your love, then he won the lottery. You hear me? He's a lucky man. Nothing else matters. You're a beautiful, smart, loving, pure woman who lights up the people around her."

A smile tugged at my lips. "Thank you."

Maryann loved me like a mother would. Growing up, she had been a great stand-in, though my mind sometimes wandered to what life would have been like under different circumstances. Until recently, I had believed my mother died in an accident. A few months ago, I discovered she was alive in a hospital in Los Angeles, though mentally vacant and incapable of most basic functions. When the media discovered the secret, they also discovered me, which was why my face was spread across TV screens throughout America.

She walked over and sat down on the swing beside me. "Don't thank me for being honest. Just calling it like I see it."

I often wondered how someone like Maryann could have gotten mixed up with my dad. She was so real. So full of life and so smart. The man she had spent most of her life with made sense. They fit. But Maryann and Kiro were a hard couple to imagine.

"You're tough, you're strong. You always have been. Even as a baby, you were so determined. Kiro adored you, but now you know he worshipped your mother. She was his light. She found the man inside no one else had ever seen and drew him out. Watching him with her amazed me. I couldn't hate her. In fact, I admired her. She was such a sweet soul, just like you. I see her in you so much. So does your dad." She stopped and squeezed my knee. "If you want this baby, then I believe you can do it. I believe you're strong enough. I've seen that strength throughout your life, and I think you can do it, but you have to embrace it. Don't let pain and fear control you, or you'll lose."

I let her words sink in and realized she was right. It was time I got strong. My baby needed it. And I needed to be strong for all of us.

Grant

"This is the fifty-seventh message. Fifty-seven days. I'm sitting here staring out at the Gulf, like I used to do with you. Nothing is the same without you here. I can't even go near the bar in my kitchen. Remembering what we did there is too difficult. Everything reminds me of you. If I could hear your voice tonight, Harlow, if I could just hear you tell me you're OK . . . I would be better. I would be able to take a deep breath. Then I'd beg. I would beg you to love me. I would beg you to forgive me. I can't—"

BEEP

I stood on my balcony staring out at the water as voice mail cut me off, then disconnected the call. Watching the waves crash over the shore used to comfort me. Now they reminded me of the fear that had started all of this. The fear that had made me say words to Harlow that she didn't deserve to hear.

Losing Jace had marked me deeper than I realized. You live your life never once thinking that when you walk away from a friend or loved one, you might never see him again. Drowning in the Gulf was the last way I expected to lose a close friend. It was unexpected and tragic, and it had changed everything for me.

I had wanted to protect myself from that kind of pain in the future. Moving on and living normally after that was impossible. Bethy, Jace's girlfriend, was proof of that. She was like a ghost now. She never smiled, and she rarely spoke. The happy gleam in her eyes was gone. I hated being near her. I hated being reminded of what could happen to all of us. She wasn't living without Jace—she was just surviving.

I let the hand holding the phone to my ear drop to my side, then tucked it into my jeans pocket and turned to go inside. Away from the water that had changed everything for me, that had changed the lives of all of Jace's close friends. None of us would ever be the same again. But I knew that I couldn't protect myself from that kind of pain. Because, like Bethy, I was just surviving now. With Harlow gone, I had no reason to smile. The pain was too much. Trying not to love her was impossible—it shattered me and brought me to my knees.

My phone started ringing, and I quickly jerked it back out of my pocket. Every time it rang, my heart started beating with the hope that it was Harlow. Rush's name appeared on the screen. As much as I wanted to smash my phone against the wall in frustration, he was still my only link to Harlow.

"Yeah," I said, closing the door and walking to my bedroom.

"I need your help. Meet me at the club as soon as possible. I'm headed that way now."

I wasn't going to the club. It was time for my nightly routine, and I didn't want to face people. "Why? I'm exhausted."

Rush muttered a curse. "Get your ass to the club. Tripp showed up, and apparently Bethy was at the bar drinking too much, and now she's yelling at him and saying all kinds of crazy shit. Blaire wanted to go, but Nate isn't feeling that great, and he wants his momma. I told her you and I would check things out and bring Bethy back to my house."

Bethy and Tripp? That didn't even make sense. Why would Bethy be yelling at Tripp? Jace had adored his cousin. Always had. There was no reason in my mind why Bethy should be mad at him. "OK. Yeah, I'll see you in a few."

"Thought so," Rush replied, then ended the call.

No one had seen Bethy do much more than move quietly through life since Jace's death. But she was drinking at the club? That didn't make any sense, either. She worked there as a cart girl. Why was she drunk at the bar? Her aunt would fire her ass without blinking an eye if she found out. Not that it would stick. Blaire would get upset and ask Rush, who was on the board of directors, to do something about it. Della wouldn't be happy, either, and seeing as how her boyfriend, Woods, owned the place—and did everything in his power to make her happy—he'd do something about it, too. But still. What the fuck was she thinking?

I grabbed my truck keys and headed out the door to deal with Bethy.

⌗

I could hear Bethy yelling the moment I stepped out of the truck, but I couldn't see where it was coming from. It was too loud to be coming from inside, so someone had to have gotten Bethy to the parking lot. I closed my truck door and followed the sound. Near the staff entrance, I saw Rush holding Bethy's arms down and talking to her. Tripp stood there, running his hands through his hair as if he wasn't sure what the hell to do.

Woods talked to him quietly, and all Tripp did was shake his head no in return.

"Come back to the house with me. Blaire wants you there. You need her right now. You also need to sober up. Tripp didn't do anything to you, Bethy. You're still grieving, and he was the closest person you could find to take it out on." Rush's voice was gentle but demanding.

"You don't know shit, Rush! Youdonknowshit!" Bethy slurred, shoving at Rush's chest. "No one knows! But he does!" she screamed, pointing a finger at Tripp. "He ruined me! He broke me. I wasn't good enough. I was never good enough! It's all his fault. He came back. Why did you come back, huh? Were you trying to hurt me? You fucking succeeded! *You* are the reason my life is hell on earth!" She was trembling now.

"Where's Della?" I asked, drawing everyone's attention to me. "Bethy needs a friend. We're just gonna upset her more like this."

Woods didn't look like he wanted Della around. He had to stop protecting her as if she was about to break. She was strong and healthy. He didn't know what fragile was. He had no idea.

"She's asleep. She's been up since five this morning," Woods said in a hard voice that meant he wasn't calling her.

"I need to leave. Seeing me upsets her. I thought I could talk to her, but she's not ready. Not yet," Tripp said. The pain in his voice was so damn obvious it hurt. He was possibly the one person who was suffering from Jace's death as much as Bethy. Why wouldn't she accept his help?

"Upset? You think I'm upset? I was fuckin' upset five years ago. Now I'm . . . lost." She said the last word in almost a whisper. Then she crumpled to the floor and wrapped her arms around her legs as she began sobbing so hard her body shook violently.

"We gotta do something. Blaire will know what to say. I should have sent Blaire and you. I just made everything worse," Rush said, looking back at me. Then he turned his attention to Tripp and stared at him a moment. "You know why she hates you, don't you?" he said in his simple, to-the-point manner.

Tripp didn't respond.

"*Yes*! He knows!" she wailed. "He knows. But Jace never knew."

Bethy's drunken ranting wasn't making any sense to me.

I hated watching this. I hated knowing that months after Jace's death, Bethy was still a broken, empty soul. Stepping around Rush, I bent down to Bethy's eye level. "I'm gonna pick you up and take you to Rush's car. He's gonna take you to Blaire, and you're gonna let her take care of you. She'll be there to listen. You can trust her. She loves you. Now, put your arm around my shoulder."

Her sad, red-rimmed eyes stared up at me for a few seconds before she put her arm around my neck. I braced one arm against her back and slid one arm under her legs and stood up with her.

"Where did you park?" I asked Rush.

"Just down there on the other side of Woods," he replied.

I glanced one last time at Tripp, who was watching Bethy with the same hopeless look I understood all too well. What didn't make sense was why Tripp was looking at Bethy like he'd move heaven and earth to take her pain away. Did they really even know each other?

Harlow

"You doing OK, sunshine?" Major asked as he took the seat beside me on the hay bale where I had sat to watch Mase work.

Glancing up at Major, I smiled, even though I didn't really feel like it. "Yes, and you?" I replied because it was the polite thing to do. I wasn't in the mood to talk to him or anyone. Not today. I had been to my weekly doctor appointment. Watching all the pregnant women and their adoring husbands in the waiting room had been hard, and it was all I could do to keep from breaking down. I missed Grant.

"Don't look like you're doing good. In fact, you look like someone killed your puppy," he said teasingly.

I knew that Maryann and Mase hadn't told Major anything. I trusted Major because he loved his family, and I was an extension of that family, but I hated people knowing before Grant. Until Grant knew about our child, I didn't want anyone else knowing. "Just having one of those days," I replied, hoping that would shut him up.

"Huh," he replied, then looked out at Mase, who was on one of the horses. "To hear the news tell it, you were hot and heavy with Grant Carter, Rush Finlay's former stepbrother. But I've been here a couple weeks, and I haven't seen the

28

guy who shoved down three reporters to get you into Rush's Range Rover and out of the public eye. You know, that clip has been played about a million times. The guy looked fierce and ready to slay dragons for you. Makes me curious about where he is now."

I had watched that clip, too. I had watched it over and over again. It was on YouTube, and I played it often. Not because it was the moment I left Grant but because Major was right. Grant looked determined and fierce. He had yelled at reporters and basically torn a path through them, from his front door to Rush's car, to get to me. But the part that I couldn't forget was the look on his face, perfectly captured by the cameras, when I had driven away. He had regretted his last words to me. The pain in his eyes had been clear, and it broke my heart and healed it all at once every time I watched the clip. He hadn't meant what he said. He had been scared.

"He doesn't know where I am," I admitted before I could stop myself.

"Really? And how is that? You hiding from him, too?"

Major was being nosy, and maybe I should have told him to mind his own business, but I didn't do that. I wanted to talk about Grant with someone. Needed to. "We needed space. He was scared of my heart condition. He doesn't want to lose me," I explained vaguely.

Major didn't respond. Instead, he reached for a piece of hay and stuck it in his mouth. With Mase's cowboy hat perched on his head and his worn-out jeans, Major looked like he belonged in Texas. He didn't look like a world traveler. I knew for a fact that he could speak three different languages fluently.

"He not trying to find you? Or call you?"

I had to delete voice mails every week so that they didn't fill up my in-box. I couldn't bring myself to listen to his voice, but I also didn't want it to become impossible for him to leave messages. "No, he calls every night. He's been trying to find me."

Major pulled the hay out of his mouth and frowned at me. "Then why you sitting here looking so sad?"

Because I missed Grant. I wanted to answer his call. I was just too scared. "I have reasons," I replied.

"You got reasons, huh? All right, then. I just hope those reasons are worth it," he replied. "I don't know if any girl could get me to leave her daily messages that go unanswered for two months. I would eventually give up and move on."

If Grant gave up, what would I do? I didn't want him to give up. But I wasn't being fair to him. I hated this. I hated having to hurt him. But if he knew, he would only be hurt more.

"Stop flirting with my sister, and get your ass out here," Mase called from the fence.

Major chuckled. "He's a little overprotective, isn't he?"

"You have no idea," I said.

Major grinned, then stood up and sauntered down to Mase as if he didn't have a care in the world.

Grant

"Message fifty-nine. Almost two months. I've never been so empty in my life. You took my soul with you. You took my heart. I'm this empty shell who goes through the motions every day, waiting for you to call me. Waiting until you answer my calls. I never imagined a life like this, but without you, I can't imagine life. You are my life. You were what was missing in my life. I was searching so hard for something to make me feel whole. I found that with you. You lit up my world and made everything so damn bright and exciting. But now you're gone, and I'm in a dark place, waiting. Needing to hear you. To touch you, To—"

BEEP

The end of another voice mail. It was the most dreaded moment of my day. The darkness in my life was so thick it was taking over everything. I had no way to see past it anymore. This voice mail was all I had to look forward to each day, because for three seconds, Harlow's voice was there, telling me to leave a message. I loved that voice. I loved those three seconds.

There was a knock on the door, followed by the doorbell. I glanced down at my phone. It was after ten. No one but Rush came by anymore, and Rush had a key. I threw back my cov-

31

ers, reached for the discarded sweatpants on the floor, then jerked them on while I walked out of the room and toward the door.

I kicked my work boots out of the way and ignored the mud that had started collecting where I left them every day. I just didn't care. My kitchen wasn't in good shape, either.

Unlocking the door, I opened it to find Woods standing on the other side. Woods Kerrington was not someone I'd expect to stop by at ten thirty at night. He had a fiancée at home he should be snuggled up to. He rarely left Della's side when he wasn't working.

"I beat Rush here. Figures. Let me in," Woods said, stepping inside, then glancing down at the dried mud on my floor. "I understand being depressed, but get a maid," he said, then headed for my living room.

I had started to ask him what the hell he was doing when headlights caught my attention, and I saw Rush's Range Rover pull in and park. What was going on?

"You got any Corona? Or just this Bud Light shit?" Woods called out from my kitchen.

I wasn't even going to respond to that question. Uppity country-club owner.

Rush climbed the steps toward me. I watched him carefully. If this was some kind of intervention, I was beating both of their asses. I needed a good fight. Some way to release the pain.

"Relax, I'm not here to council you. Unclench your fists, and let me inside. I have something you need to hear," Rush said as he stopped in front of me.

"Why is Woods here?" I asked, not sure I believed him.

Rush sighed and rubbed his chin. He was nervous. Shit. What did he need to tell me? "I just thought we might need some backup. What I'm gonna tell you isn't something you're gonna want to hear. But you need to know. So I have him here in case you react badly."

"Is Harlow OK?" I asked, grabbing his arm as he stepped into the apartment. The instant panic that swamped me gave me the most helpless feeling I'd ever had.

"She's fine. Let go and calm down. Let's go in the living room," Rush said, then shot a pointed look at my grip on his arm. I let go, and he walked past me. If Harlow was OK, I didn't see how anything else could upset me. She was it for me. I didn't care about anything or anyone else. Rush knew that, so his statement that Harlow was OK didn't do much to ease my mind.

I stalked after him and found Woods on my sofa with a beer and one leg propped up on the ottoman, watching me. His eyes swung to Rush's, then back to me. He didn't look like he knew what this was about, either. The curiosity in his gaze wasn't the same concerned look in Rush's.

"Thanks for meeting me here," Rush said, and Woods nodded his head.

"No problem. It sounded important," Woods replied.

"Tell me what the fuck is going on," I demanded, not willing to wait any longer. I wasn't going to calm down, and I sure as hell wasn't going to sit down.

Rush turned around to look at me. "Probably should sit down," he said.

"No," I barked.

"Didn't think so, but I thought I'd try," he replied. He didn't move to sit down, either. "Mase called me about two hours ago," he began, then ran his hand through his hair, which was a nervous habit of his.

"Is she with Mase now?" I asked, scanning the room for where I'd left my keys when I got home from work earlier. If she was in Texas, I would get on the next flight out.

"Grant. No. Stop. Listen to me," Rush said in a sharp tone.

I swung my gaze back to his. "If she is in Texas, I'm going to motherfucking Texas! You can't stop me. The cops can't stop me. No one CAN. FUCKING. STOP. ME!" I roared.

"You need to listen to what I have to say first. It's important." Rush's tone had turned commanding. Thing was, I didn't give a rat's ass. I was going to see Harlow.

"She can tell me what's going on. I'm going to Texas," I told him with enough determination that he knew I was serious. I had to get to her.

"There are things you need to know," he said, raising his voice over mine.

"All I need to know is where she is. That's all I need to fucking know!" I snarled. He was wasting my time. I had to get my keys and get out of here.

"Oh, for Christ's sake! I didn't want to just come out and lay this on you, but you're so fucking stubborn!" he yelled as I turned away from him. "She's pregnant. Harlow is pregnant, and she won't get an abortion, and giving birth could . . ."

He didn't finish. He didn't have to. I knew what the rest of that sentence was. My knees gave way, and I grabbed the back of the chair in front of me while sheer terror squeezed my lungs and heart until I couldn't take a breath.

Harlow couldn't be pregnant. She couldn't be. Oh, God, no.

I couldn't lose her. I needed her to live. Even if she wouldn't talk to me, I needed her alive on this earth.

"Mase is worried. She's determined to have this child. Mase said she refuses to tell you because she knows you won't agree with her. You'll want her to get an abortion. She's unwilling to even consider it."

"No. She can't do this. I can't lose her," I said, shaking my head, refusing to accept this. I had to get to Texas. I grabbed my keys and headed for the door.

"Where are you going?" Rush called out.

"Texas."

"I didn't say she was there. I said I'd talked to Mase," Rush said as he came after me.

"Then where is she? I won't lose her. She can't do this." I was yelling so loudly that Rush couldn't help wincing.

"You need a plan," Rush said, grabbing my arm in a firm grip. "Mase told me more. If you'll sit and calm your ass down, I can tell you everything. Being prepared is the only way you can get through to her."

He was right. I hated waiting. I hated not being able to get to her, but he was right. I had to be levelheaded. If I was going to save her, I had to be ready when I saw her. Going after her in a wild panic wasn't going to do anything but send her running to a new hiding place.

"Does she feel OK? Did he say if she was healthy? Is she sick?" I asked.

"She's fine. Mase is keeping her close. Other than missing you, she's doing OK."

She missed me? All she had to do was call me. I'd be there. But then, why would she trust me? After what I'd done to her.

The self-hatred inside me grew and twisted into an ugly ball of fury. I could be with her right now if I'd handled it right. If I hadn't been so selfish and scared. She wouldn't be facing this alone right now.

"I call . . . I call every damn day. All she has to do is answer."

Rush patted me on the back. "She's scared, too. She's just scared for different reasons."

How could she even consider this? Her heart . . . she was so fragile. "I don't understand why she would do this. She knows she can't."

Rush sank into the leather chair close to him and let out a weary sigh. "The baby is real to her. It's inside her. She has a connection with it already. It's a mother thing. I can't say that I know how you feel, because the moment I found out Blaire was pregnant, I wanted that baby. It was our baby. It was a part of us. But Blaire was connected to Nate. Even then. I don't think I felt quite what she felt until they put him in my arms. And . . ." Rush paused and shook his head, then looked directly at me. "I could never choose between Nate and Blaire. Now that I have him, I couldn't comprehend not having him. Giving him up. And if Harlow feels even a small portion of that already, I get it. I understand completely."

His situation had been different. Completely different. He had never had to face the possibility of Blaire dying. God! I couldn't even think about it. It hurt too damn bad. "You," I said, pointing at him. "You have no idea what this feels like. You were never faced with losing Blaire. Of her . . ." I couldn't say it aloud. It would shatter me.

"You're right. I never faced it. I know that if Blaire had been in the same situation, I would have wanted her to get an abortion. I wouldn't have wanted her to take a chance with her life. She's my world. But now . . . I can't imagine a world without Nate in it. He—" Rush stopped and took a deep breath. "Nate completes my world."

This didn't matter. I would never hold that child, because nothing was more important than Harlow's life. Her heart would keep beating. I would make damn sure of it. "You're saying I have to choose. Well, I choose Harlow."

Rush nodded. "I know. But she chooses that baby. She has that connection already. I understand her fierce need to protect her baby . . . *your* baby."

Shaking my head, I walked away from him. Away from Woods, who had remained silent on the sofa. The urge to throw things and curse the world was beating in my chest, wanting out. I couldn't do that now, though. Focusing on Harlow and saving her was my priority—not losing my shit.

"I wouldn't let Della do it, either," Woods finally spoke. I turned back to look at him. "I wouldn't let her sacrifice her life. I'm nothing without her. I get it. You have to save her."

Woods would never be in my position, but at least he understood. I wasn't a monster for wanting Harlow to abort my child. Her body couldn't handle it. She wasn't meant to give birth. This was my fault. I hadn't been careful enough.

"I'm not saying I don't understand. I'm just saying I also understand Harlow. The love you have for your child is intense. Go easy on her. Don't force her. If you do, she'll run away. You won't be able to save her," Rush said, then stood up. "Mase has a house at the back of his parents' ranch. It's off the road, and you have to go through his parents' front gate to get back there. That's where she's staying. She's been hiding there all along. I was good with keeping her secret until Mase called me today and told me about the pregnancy. I talked to Blaire, and she said it was time I told you. Mase wants you to go and talk to her. He can't talk her out of it, and he needs your help. He also said she's lost weight and hasn't cracked a smile. She's missing you, but she's staying away from you because she's also protecting you. She doesn't want you to try to stop her." Rush paused and glanced back at Woods, then turned back to me. "And she doesn't want you to be afraid."

My fear of losing her. She was keeping me from my nightmare come to life. "I'm going to Texas tonight. I can't stay away from her any longer."

Rush nodded. "I know. I figured that out already. I have a private plane waiting for you at the airport. Just be smart. Know that she'll defend that child before anything else. Be sensitive, because acting as if that life inside her means nothing to you will wound her. It's a part of you that she's carrying. That makes her love it even more."

Harlow

My eyes flew open, and it took me a moment to figure out why I was awake before the sun was up. Deep voices coming from outside snapped me out of my sleepy thoughts, and I sat up in bed and listened. Reaching for my phone, I saw it was just after three in the morning. I jumped out of the large four-poster bed, grabbed my wrap, and tugged it on before heading for the front door toward the voices.

Glancing over at Mase's bedroom door, I saw that it was open and the light was on. One of those voices outside belonged to Mase. If his father or Major was here this early, then something must be wrong down at the ranch. I tied the wrap closed with the silky belt that hung at my waist and slipped my feet into a pair of furry slippers that I had left by my bedroom door last night when I had come inside after swinging on the front porch.

Stepping out onto the dark landing of the stairs, it was hard to see. The voices were to the right of the porch. I started to walk toward them but paused at the top of the stairs when Grant's familiar voice stopped me.

"I want to see her now. Just let me in. I won't disturb her, I'll just watch her sleep. I swear. I'm begging you, please let me see her." The desperation in his voice was more than I could handle. I had ignored his phone calls and stayed away from him for almost two months.

"She doesn't need to be surprised like this. She's fragile right now, and—"

"I know she's fragile. *God*! Do you think I'd do anything to hurt her? I would rather throw myself off a fucking cliff, Mase. I hurt her once, and I swear to God, I'll never do it again. Just let me in there. Let me see her. Please, I need to be close to her."

There was a pause. Even through the darkness, I could see Grant's eyes as they locked on me. He stepped around Mase and started walking toward me. There was determination in his eyes, but there was also so much pain. I had caused that pain. Sure, he'd hurt me, but he'd done everything to contact me, to try to find me. He hadn't just let me go.

"Harlow." He said my name in such a reverent tone that my knees wobbled and my body felt weak. Relief washed through me. Relief I hadn't been expecting. He was here, and I wasn't going to be able to push him away. And I was relieved because I needed him. More than anyone on this earth, I needed him.

"You came," I said simply.

He climbed the stairs, taking them two at a time until he was in front of me. "I'd have been here sooner if I knew where you were. I looked for you. I called." He stopped searching my face for answers.

I would have to tell him, and he would leave when he understood the gamble. But right now, I needed him. I wasn't ready to tell him about the baby and send him running away in fear.

"We're going to go to my room, Mase," I told my brother, glancing around Grant to see Mase watching us cautiously from the bottom of the steps.

He nodded and stayed where he was. Turning back to Grant, I slipped my hand in his and led him toward my room. I had missed him, and my emotions were all over the place. I didn't trust myself to do or say the right thing. I just wanted him close to me. With his arms around me, I would feel like everything was OK.

Grant stayed so close to my side that his body brushed mine as we walked into the bedroom. He closed the door behind us, then pulled me tightly into his arms. We just stood there in the darkness. I wrapped my arms around his waist and laid my head on his chest. The strength from having him with me again like this was unexpected. My heart had always been weak, but loving Grant made it strong.

His lips brushed the top of my head. "I love you. I love you so much," he whispered into the silence.

The fullness inside from hearing those words made me feel as if I would burst. I had this man's love. Deep down, I'd known he loved me, but hearing him say that after everything I had put him through made it real.

"I love you, too," I told him, then tilted my head back and stared up into his eyes. The emotion in those depths rocked me.

"You need to sleep. We can talk in the morning, but right now, you need to rest, and I want nothing more than to hold you while you do," he said, then pressed a kiss on my forehead as if I were a delicate flower he didn't want to break.

I didn't want to sleep. There was a lot I wanted to do, but sleeping wasn't one of them. "I'm awake now," I told him.

He cupped my face with one hand and brushed his thumb over my cheek. "You should be asleep. I woke you up. You need sleep before we talk. I need some sleep, too."

He picked me up, carried me over to the bed, and placed me on it before reaching for his shirt and tugging it off. I watched in wonder as his beautiful chest was revealed. He pulled off his shoes and went to unbutton his jeans and stopped. My gaze had been completely wrapped up in watching him undress, so when he didn't continue, I lifted my eyes to meet his.

Instead of hunger, I saw pain. I didn't understand.

"I think I'll leave these on. We need to sleep," he said, then climbed onto the bed and lay back, gently pulling me toward his chest. His arms encircled me.

"I'm almost scared to close my eyes," I admitted.

"Why?" he asked, tensing underneath me.

I tucked my head back against his shoulder so I could see his face. "Because I'm afraid this is a dream. I'll wake up, and you won't be here," I admitted, then reached up and touched his face to remind myself that he was real and he was here.

"If you wake up and this is a dream, call me. I'll come running. I swear," he said, then took my hand and kissed my palm. "All you ever have to do is call me, and I will drop anything to be with you."

Grant

I had woken up more than an hour ago, but Harlow was still sleeping peacefully, so I wasn't moving. She needed sleep. Her body needed all the rest it could get until I could make her see reason. I glanced down at her curled up beside me and noticed her hand resting protectively over her stomach. Even in her sleep, she was protecting the life inside her.

A tug inside me at the idea of a baby, my baby, startled me. I didn't expect to feel anything for the life that could take her from me. But I did. I felt something. It wasn't enough to bargain with Harlow's life, but I felt a deep sense of loss when I thought about what we had to do. I couldn't pretend it wasn't there. I would mourn the baby, but I would be able to move on because I would have Harlow.

Convincing Harlow that saving herself was most important was my main focus. That and keeping her rested and her body healthy. I just didn't know yet how hard that first part was going to be. From the way Rush talked, it wouldn't be easy.

The smell of coffee drifted into the room, and I heard Mase moving around in the small cabin. I wanted him to leave— do something else and leave us alone. I didn't need his interference. This was between Harlow and me. Her brother had taken care of her when I couldn't, but I was here now, and it was time he stepped down.

"Good morning." Harlow's sleepy voice brought my gaze back to her face. Those big, beautiful eyes of hers looked happy this morning. She wanted me here. She may have been trying to keep me away, but she wanted me here. That was all the proof I needed.

"Morning, sweet girl," I replied, then pressed a kiss to her soft lips. I was gentle and didn't push for more. We needed to talk first. Tasting her would have to wait. I wasn't sure I could remain focused if I let myself take too much right now.

"It wasn't a dream," she whispered.

"No. It was real. I'm here," I assured her. And I wasn't leaving without her.

She began tracing small shapes on my stomach with her fingertip. I watched her small hand and the frown starting to pucker her forehead. She was thinking. I knew what about. She wasn't sure what to do now that I was here.

I didn't doubt that she was aware of the fact that I wasn't leaving her. Letting her worry and stress wasn't good for her. I reached down and took her hand in mine and squeezed it. I had to ease into this, and I had to choose my words with caution.

"I can't lose you. It would destroy me. You might as well take me with you. I won't be able to live if you don't." I stopped and fought the terror that came with those thoughts. I shoved it away, because I refused to accept it. "I want you to be happy, but I want you alive. I'll give you anything. Just ask. But I can't sacrifice you. Your life isn't something I'm willing to gamble with."

She had gone still in my arms, so still I wasn't sure if she was even breathing. It hadn't dawned on her that I could already know her secret. If she even thought of running from me, I'd chase her down.

"You came into my life. You changed my world. You made me realize I'm capable of loving completely. You're my one. You're it. This is my epic love, and I can't lose that."

Harlow let out a shaky breath and buried her face in my chest. I cupped the back of her head with my hand and gently stroked her back as she took several deep breaths. Giving up on her wasn't something I would ever do. She just had to understand my devotion and my need for her. "When did you become such a sweet-talker? Prepare a girl before you say stuff like that," she said as she lifted her head to look at me. The redness in her eyes and the unshed tears made me want to cuddle her and take her away from anything that could hurt her.

"It's true," I assured her.

She closed her eyes and let out a long, uneven breath. "All my life, I've dreamed of having someone love me like you do. But in that dream, I imagined a family. The kind I didn't get to have as a kid. A husband who loved me and our kids, because I always wanted kids. I've watched Rush hold Nate, and the joy in his eyes is something I always wanted for myself. I never thought I'd experience either of those things. But I was given this wonderful gift of you"—she paused and touched her flat stomach again—"and I was given this miracle. One I didn't plan on or expect, but I got it all the same. I can't end this. I can't . . . I can't. I love you, but I can't."

Rush had been right. She loved the life inside her already.

She didn't even know the child, but she loved it. She loved it enough to give her life for it. How could reason compete with that? How could I save her from this?

Pulling her up against my chest tightly, I held her in my arms and breathed her in. I understood what she wanted, but it couldn't be this way. I could love her for the rest of our lives, but carrying a child and giving birth were too dangerous.

I was going to have to put a stop to this. I just didn't know how. I did know that pushing it right now was not the right thing to do. I needed to restore the faith she had in me. I had to fix us first. Then I would show her how she couldn't do this to me—how leaving me would destroy my life. I'd never recover from losing her. Never.

"Who told you?" she asked in a soft whisper. She had trusted her brother to keep her secret, but I couldn't lie to her. I figured Mase would willingly admit it, anyway.

"Mase called Rush," I explained. "He's worried about you. Scared enough to call me. Don't be mad at him. I owe him my life now."

Harlow let out a long sigh and pressed a kiss to my chest before replying. "I'm not mad at him. I woke up in your arms. How can I be mad at him for that?"

Damn, I didn't deserve her. Not even a little.

"Smells like he made coffee. You want some?" she asked, wiggling closer to me.

There were a lot of things I wanted to do with her at the moment, but I knew I wasn't going to do anything until I'd spoken to a doctor. I needed to know what was safe and what wasn't. I had to protect her. If she wasn't going to take care of herself, I would. "Yeah, let's get some coffee," I replied, then pressed a kiss to the top of her head.

Her puckered lips were tempting, and she seemed a bit frustrated that I wasn't giving in to them, but I didn't know how smart it was to kiss her while we were in bed like this. What if she pushed for more? Could I tell her no, and if I didn't, would it hurt her? I moved out of her arms before she could tempt me any more and moved away from her.

"I want to talk to your doctor. Today. As soon as abso-fucking-lutely possible," I told her.

She sat up and let the covers fall to her waist. The flimsy excuse for clothing she had worn to bed—with no bra—didn't help. At all. "Is that what's bothering you?" she asked, seeming almost relieved and a little amused. "I had an appointment yesterday, but I didn't ask about . . . that. I didn't think about it being a possibility," she said, a smile playing on her lips.

"Get dressed, and let's get some coffee. Wait—can you even drink coffee? Is that safe?" There were so many things I hadn't thought about, that I didn't know. I needed a damn class on how to keep Harlow safe and healthy. The helpless feeling I got every time I thought about not being able to save her was beginning to control me already.

"Mase will have made me some decaf," she assured me as she stood up. Even with the terror of physically hurting her haunting me, my body still reacted to seeing her like this. All sexy and rumpled from sleep. I had to get out of this room.

"OK, I'll meet you out there for breakfast," I said, and left the room before she could persuade me to give in and kiss her.

Harlow

I sat back down on the bed and stared at the door Grant had escaped through. He was terrified. It was all over his face and in his actions. When I had seen his face this morning, I had been so happy that I hadn't thought about his reaction to the news. I had just needed him to hold me. I had wanted him to tell me he would stand by me in this. I had wanted to dream about the family we would have. But the man who had just bolted from the room without even properly kissing me was not going to be capable of fulfilling all of those things.

Of course, Mase was the reason Grant had found out. Mase was scared, too, and calling Rush had been his last hope. I understood that. What Mase didn't get was that I couldn't make this decision to soothe Grant's fears. The truth was, I was scared, too, but that didn't change anything. Life was full of fears, and running from those fears would keep us from experiences that make life worth living. This baby was a gift— one I would protect.

Dealing with Grant was another thing. I didn't want him to leave me. I didn't want to stay here and be a burden to my brother. But just because I didn't want to do something, that didn't mean I wouldn't if I had to. Love shouldn't make our choices for us; it should just add importance to our choices. Explaining that to Grant and my brother was something I didn't know how to do.

I would give Grant time to accept this, but if he couldn't, then I would have to leave again, this time to the safety of my dad's house in L.A. Even if it was the last place I wanted to be.

The front door to the house opened, and another male voice joined the others in the kitchen. Major was here. He'd made it a habit to have coffee with us ever since Maryann sent him over with biscuits and gravy on his first morning at the ranch. The bully from my childhood was actually quite a charming guy now. A bit of a player—OK, a serious player—but I wasn't dating him, so I enjoyed his company.

I quickly changed into a pair of cutoff sweats and a long-sleeved T-shirt before walking into the living room and kitchen area. The house was small, so these two areas flowed into each other in one large, open space. The stone fireplace in the living room gave the place a homey feel.

All three men stopped talking and turned to look at me. Grant's eyes quickly took in my clothing, and he looked pleased. I wasn't sure why. Maybe it was because he was just happy to be with me. He stood up and walked over to me and pulled me into his arms as if we hadn't just been in bed together. "I was about to come check on you," he whispered as he pressed a kiss to my temple.

"Don't do that in front of me. I got you here, Grant, so at least respect the fact that I don't want to see your PDA. All it does is remind me of that plane ride I took with the two of you. Not something I want to think about," Mase grumbled as he frowned up at us. He was sitting across the table with his legs stretched out in front of him and his feet crossed at the ankles. I blushed at the memory of my brother overhearing Grant and me having sex on a private plane to L.A.

"Good morning to you, too," I replied, glad that Grant hadn't let me go just because of my grumpy brother.

Mase only grunted in return.

"No good morning for me, beautiful?" Major asked with the lazy grin he knew made women everywhere want to please him. He knew I was completely unaffected by him, which made it even more ridiculous that he would flash that smile on me now. Grant's arms tightened around me, and I felt him tense. He didn't know Major was a world-class flirt and meant nothing by it.

"Morning, Major," I replied, snuggling further into Grant's arms to reassure him. "I see you've met . . . Grant," I finished weakly. I wasn't sure how I was supposed to refer to Grant. "Baby daddy" didn't seem appropriate.

"Yep, Mase introduced me to him already. I hadn't real-ized you had a man. I'm dealing with the heartbreak at the moment," he replied with that stupid grin. That wasn't true— I had confessed my feelings for Grant to Major on that hay bale just a few days ago. He was trying to cause trouble. I had started to scold him when Grant loosened his hold on me to take a step toward Major. I reached out to grab his arm, though Major kind of deserved it.

"Oh, for fuck's sake, dickhead. Stop teasing Grant. The man's about to beat the shit out of you, and I'm gonna let him. Drink your coffee, and shut the hell up, or leave," Mase said, clearly annoyed with Major's flirting.

I wrapped both of my hands around Grant's arm. "He

knows about you. He's just teasing." I wanted to add that I was pregnant with his baby. He shouldn't be acting possessive, but he also didn't need a reminder of our real issues right now.

Major held up his hands. "Didn't mean to cause a problem. No one warned me Grant was so damn territorial."

Mase rolled his eyes and shook his head at his cousin's words, then looked at me. "You OK?" he asked, his tone shifting from annoyed to sincere. I knew what he meant. He had called Rush knowing it would send Grant straight to me. He was making sure he'd done the right thing. I could be mad at him for not respecting my wishes, but Grant's arms were around me again, and just feeling his warmth made me feel stronger.

"Yes," I replied honestly. I was happy. I was happier than I had been in two months. And I wasn't scared. Not anymore. Just seeing Grant and knowing we had created life inside me reminded me how much I loved this baby.

"Wish I'd known sooner," Grant said in a tense voice, and I glanced up at him to see that he was frowning at Mase.

"He was obeying my wishes. He wanted me to call you. He begged me to answer your calls every night." I didn't want Grant mad at my brother for doing what I had asked. I needed them to be a family. And not just for me.

"She's stubborn," Mase added.

Grant bent his head toward mine. "I know," was his only response.

I was standing right there while they talked about me. Instead of being snarky, I just shrugged. I *was* stubborn. I was determined. It was part of my strength. I wouldn't deny that. I was proud of it.

"So what's the plan?" Mase asked.

"Plan? What kind of plan?" Major piped up after watching us quietly.

I turned my head toward Grant. "He doesn't know," I explained to him in a whisper.

"Not your business," Mase informed Major.

"I'm feeling slightly unwelcome in this little gathering. I think I'll head on down to the stables and get things going. See you later," Major said to Mase, then glanced over at me and smiled. "First time I've seen you really smile. Looks good on you," he said, and he winked before leaving the house in a few long strides.

"Don't get all possessive, Grant. He's right. She hasn't smiled in the last few months, then you show up here and she's all smiles this morning. It's a relief," Mase said, standing up from the table. "I know you have plans, and I want to know what they are." Although his eyes glanced down at me briefly, he was talking to Grant. I hadn't had time to think about plans or discuss things with him. I wasn't sure he had any plans yet. I didn't want him to have any. We needed time.

"Rush made some calls. There's a doctor back in Destin who specializes in high-risk pregnancies. Specifically what we are dealing with here. He's one of the best. I'm taking her home—to my home, to our home—now."

Whoa. Wait. What? I stepped out of his embrace and crossed my arms over my chest. As much as I wanted to be with Grant, I didn't like the idea of leaving the comfort zone I had found here. I was free to make my own decisions, and I had Maryann's support.

Grant's eyes were on me, and the pleading in them almost

had me buckling without even considering the outcome. "We can't live with your brother, and I can't live without you. I want you with the best doctors, sweet girl. Please, come back with me. Let me keep you safe."

Mase cleared his throat, but I didn't turn away from Grant. "As much as I like having you here, I hate seeing you look so lost. He's what you want. But I'll come to Rosemary Beach any time you need me. All you have to do is call, and I'll come get you. I don't care who I have to fight to get to you." That was Mase's way of warning Grant that he was still on my side. But I didn't want there to be sides.

Grant reached out and cupped my face with his hands. "Let me take you home. I will do it right this time. Give me one more chance. I swear, I'll make it right."

There were so many reasons leaving was a bad idea. But at that moment, none of them mattered.

"OK," I replied.

Grant

While Harlow packed her things and said her good-byes to Maryann, I set up a doctor's appointment for the next day with the ob-gyn in Destin whom Rush had found. The doctor was a member of the Kerrington Country Club, and a call from Woods had magically opened up his appointment calendar for us.

I wasn't going to push her to do anything she didn't want to do right now. My first plan was to get her back home and settled in. I needed to hear what the doctor had to say about her health, and then . . . then I would talk to her, convince her that she couldn't gamble with her life. She was too precious to me.

She had gone down to Mase's parents' house an hour ago, but I didn't want to interrupt her or make her feel like I was rushing her. I sent a text to Rush to let him know Woods had helped me get an appointment and to thank him for doing some research for me. Then I sat down and turned on the television.

The first thing that filled the screen was Kiro Manning's face. Two months ago, news that Harlow's mother was still alive had been covered by every media outlet. After the first few weeks, with no sighting of Harlow or Kiro, the news was slowly forgotten. Then photos of Kiro as he pushed Emily—Harlow's mother—in a wheelchair by the private lake behind her nursing home had surfaced.

When Kiro saw the photos, he had beaten the hell out of the security guards at the nursing home, which had also made the news. The security guards hadn't pressed charges, and Kiro was free to go. Then, just when *that* piece of news had begun to fade, Slacker Demon announced that they were canceling the rest of their tour. Kiro wasn't willing to finish it. He hadn't been seen again. The world was going crazy, afraid they had heard the last of Slacker Demon.

Now they were showing photos of Kiro at parties from earlier that year, before the news that his wife was still alive had leaked. I hated that Harlow had to see this shit. She had enough to worry about—she didn't need this, too. The only good thing was that they had stopped discussing Harlow.

"She's on her way. Turn that off," Mase said as he entered the house.

I turned it off and stood up. "She ever watch this stuff?" I asked, hoping she had stayed away from it.

He shrugged. "Not much. She misses Kiro. She'd never admit it, but she worries over him. She's the one he loved, and she loves him, too. She doesn't like knowing he's suffered all these years over her mother. But right now, her main concern is the . . . baby."

The baby. *Our baby.* It didn't seem real. I forced thoughts of it out of my head. I couldn't think about that right now. I had to stay focused and get Harlow back home. I wanted to wrap her up and protect her. Getting her back to my place was the first step.

"You don't want her to have it, do you?" Mase asked with a scowl on his face.

"I want Harlow," I replied. That was all that mattered.

"She wants the baby."

I knew that. I just didn't want to talk about it right now. "I'm going to handle that. I just need time."

Mase nodded and let out a weary sigh. "You've got to. I can't lose her, either. I love that girl, too."

"We won't lose her. I won't let that happen," I assured him, but I was assuring myself just as much.

A truck came up the driveway, and I watched as Harlow stepped out of Maryann's truck and waved good-bye to her. Then she turned to the house and headed our way. A small smile played on her lips, and she looked happy. I loved seeing her happy.

"You make her smile," Mase said. "That's the only reason I'm letting her leave with you. I think you might be the only other person on this earth who wants her alive as much as I do."

I wasn't going to tell him that there was no way he could want her healthy and alive more than me. He had no idea what it was like for a girl to be someone's whole reason for breathing.

She opened the screen door, and her gaze swung to me as her lips pulled up into a full smile. "I'm ready," she said.

"You gonna hug me before you go?" Mase asked from across the room.

Harlow smiled and walked over to him. "Of course. I wouldn't leave without telling you good-bye and thank you. For everything." She wrapped her arms around him as he held her close. His eyes found me over her head. He didn't have to say it out loud for me to understand his warning. If I ever hurt her again, he'd kill me. But there was no reason for him to be worried about that. I would walk on water for that woman.

"Call me if you need anything," Mase told her.

"I will. Love you," she said, then stepped back out of his embrace.

"Love you, too," he said.

They had a normal kind of sibling love, where they truly cared for each other and weren't selfish. I thought about what Rush had with Nan, which was very one-sided. Nan was too selfish to appreciate her brother. I wished Rush had something like this. He deserved it.

"Let's go home," she said as she turned back to me.

Home. That had meant a lot of different things to me all my life. But now anywhere she was with me would be home.

Harlow

He wouldn't talk about it. Not one time had he brought it up. It was like waiting for the other shoe to drop. I had told him I wouldn't abort the baby, and now we were just quietly sitting on the plane.

He hadn't asked about the baby at all since I'd told him, and other than a quick kiss before we drove to the airport, he only tried to hold me—nothing more. He wasn't acting like the passionate, take-control man who had introduced me to intimacy. It was like I was made of blown glass; he was handling me as if one wrong move would break me.

Which was why I hadn't wanted to tell him about my heart in the first place.

I hated being treated differently, but things were worse now. I wasn't just a sick girl to him; I was also the girl who was hanging on by a thread. Did he not get that I was alive because I refused to give in to the restrictions of my heart condition? I had been a fighter since the day I was born. I wasn't about to stop now.

I wanted my Grant back. The man who couldn't keep his hands off me. The man who I knew wanted me above all things and made me feel desired. Not the man who acted like it was his one goal in life to keep me alive. That was not what I wanted at all.

"You OK?" His concerned voice only fueled my frustration.

I shrugged, because I was afraid that if I opened my mouth, I would yell at him. I loved him, and I was happy to be with him, so I didn't want to yell at him. But I wasn't sure I could keep from doing just that if he kept this up.

"You're frowning like something's bothering you," he pointed out.

Something *was* bothering me, but I wasn't going to share that with him. I bit down on my bottom lip to keep from growling in frustration and turned to look out the plane window. We were close to Destin, Florida, now. I could see the ocean.

"Harlow." His voice was gentle. "Look at me, please."

I hated it when I tried to be firm and he went all sweet. It was hard to ignore a sweet Grant Carter. Giving in, I glanced over at him. His forehead was creased in a frown, and his eyes looked full of worry. "I'm not breakable. I'm still me. You're treating me differently," I said, hating the way my voice cracked, which only made me seem more vulnerable. I was trying to convince this man that I was tough.

Grant stood up from the seat across from me and moved to the leather sofa beside me, pulling me into his arms. He let out a weary sigh and kissed the top of my head. I had expected him to immediately deny that he had been treating me differently, but he wasn't doing that. At least he was aware of it.

"I'm sorry. I'm trying to deal with this right now. All I can think about is keeping you safe."

"I've been taking care of myself all my life. I'm not fragile. I want to be treated like . . . like how you treated me before." I couldn't make myself say I wanted him to want me. That just sounded pathetic.

"I don't know if I can do that," he replied.

I hadn't realized that just a few words could be so heart-breaking.

"Give me time. After we talk to the doctor, I'll feel like I have some control over this. I can't just disregard your health because I want you. Don't doubt for a moment that all I can think about is stripping you down and making love to you over and over again. Hearing you pant and cry out. I crave that, baby. But you're my world. I protect what's mine."

How could I argue with that? I wrapped my arms around him and buried my face in his chest. We were going to get through this. He was here with me, and he wasn't running scared. He wanted me safe, and I couldn't be mad about that. Grant had his fears. I had to respect those and give him time. "I missed you," I said against his chest, although he already knew that. I wanted to tell him again.

"I missed you more. Every damn second I missed you," he said as his lips hovered close to my ear. The warmth from his breath caused me to shiver.

We sat there in each other's arms for the rest of the flight. We didn't talk, because we didn't need to. Just being together was enough. My eyes began to grow heavy, and I closed them, knowing that when I woke up, he'd be there.

⌗

As we walked into the doctor's office in Destin, Grant was holding my hand. This time, when I saw the other pregnant women in the waiting room with their husbands, I didn't feel a sense of loss or sadness. Grant was with me, hovering over me in all his possessive, protective glory, as if he needed to fight off an attack of some sort. He was adorable.

"Go sit down, and I'll get the paperwork to fill out," he said gently as he pointed to the empty chairs across the room.

I didn't argue with him, because I was beginning to realize he needed to do this. It made him feel safer if he was taking care of me. Even if I could get my own paperwork. I walked over to my seat and noticed that the eyes of several other females in the room were all directed toward Grant. Of course they were. He stood out. His low voice as he spoke to the lady at the check-in desk was enough to catch anyone's attention. But the view of his backside in those jeans was also very hard to look away from. The lady closest to him sat up straighter and crossed her legs. She also adjusted her bra, pushing her boobs up so that her cleavage was hard to miss. A flash of anger shot through me, and I felt my face get hot. I glared at her as she kept her attention completely trained on Grant. She flipped her long blond hair over her shoulder and tugged her skirt up just a little so more of her thigh was showing. What the hell?

Grant turned around with the clipboard, and his gaze instantly found mine. For a moment, I felt better. Then the blonde's voice stopped him.

"Grant Carter?" she cooed in a sultry voice that couldn't have been her real voice. Grant stopped and glanced back at the woman who had fixed herself up for his attention. He paused and then smiled. My stomach felt sick.

"Melody?" he replied, as if he wasn't sure if that was her name or not.

She beamed up at him like he had said the most wonderful thing in the world. I was officially nauseated. And I was jealous. Completely jealous. Because he was smiling at her. "What are you doing here? Never expected to see Grant Carter at my gyno's office." As if she hadn't seen him walk in with me.

Grant turned to me, and his grin grew. "I'm here with my . . ." He paused. It was only a brief pause, but in that moment, it felt like he had sliced me with a knife. He didn't even know what I was to him. He hadn't thought about it. "Girlfriend," he finished, before winking at me and turning back to Blondie with the big boobs.

Blondie barely glanced my way, and then she did a double take. When I walked next to Grant in a room full of women, no one paid attention to me, so I hadn't been recognized. I hated that my face was so well known now.

"Is that . . . oh, my God, it is," she said in a surprised voice.

Grant moved fast. He was in front of me, taking my hand and pulling me up against him in seconds, moving me toward the door leading out of the waiting room. "She needs privacy," he informed the lady at the desk, and she seemed to understand completely and nodded as he closed the door behind us.

A nurse met us in the empty hallway. "This way," she said as she opened a door to an exam room and waved for us to go inside. "Have Miss Manning fill out the paperwork, and I'll be back shortly to get it." I was a little dizzy from how quickly that had happened. Grant had moved fast. He hadn't taken time to say good-bye to Melody or make any explanations.

"Sorry. I should have known she'd recognize you. She's the fangirl sort. I brought her around Rush once, and she acted like an idiot," Grant said, looking frustrated.

"So you dated her?" I asked, unable to help the jealous tone in my voice. I normally wasn't so transparent with my emotions, but I couldn't seem to stop myself.

Grant frowned, and then a small smile tugged on the corners of his lips. He closed the space between us and backed me up against the exam table as he towered over me, looking extremely pleased. "Yeah, I dated her a few times years ago. You jealous, sweet girl?" he asked with a sugary, warm drawl.

I could have lied, but instead, I shrugged. I would try for nonchalance.

Grant threw his head back and laughed before caging me in with both of his arms as he leaned down over me. "Oh, no, you don't get to do that. I am enjoying this moment. I like that you got jealous of me. Not that you have anything to be jealous of ever, but I like it. I'm yours, baby, but knowing you want me makes it pretty damn sweet."

I tried to frown, but a giggle escaped.

Grant

"We'll need to take this one step at a time. Harlow has been made aware of the risks. I see women with her condition deliver babies several times a year. But then, I also see other things happen. While maternal mortality has decreased in the last decade, that's still our number one concern here. Then there's the possibility that the fetus won't make it past the first trimester. A spontaneous abortion or miscarriage could occur, which we can't control—it happens even in normal pregnancies. But it could cause complications. Alternatively, the baby could come early. And if the birth is successful, the baby could inherit Harlow's condition."

The doctor was talking, and I was hearing him, but I was losing focus. The term "maternal mortality" had seized my lungs and caused my heart to slam against my rib cage. I couldn't accept those two words. Ever.

The doctor directed his next words at Harlow. "Weekly visits are a must. I have to monitor your heart rate, and as we progress, we will need to keep an eye on the fetus as it matures."

Fucking complications. I hated this. I fucking hated it, knowing that Harlow was facing these dangers because I didn't use a damn condom a couple of times. This was my fault. If I lost her, it would all be on me. I did this to her. I put that . . . that baby in there that she was so determined to protect. That she loved.

I loved her. I loved her so damn much.

"I went over your records this morning as soon as the fax came in. I'm pleased to say that you're in much better health than most women with this condition. You had successful surgeries as a child, and you have been healthy. No problems or issues. You are high-risk, but all the signs tell me we can do this. You're a fighter. That much is obvious, from what I've seen." The doctor looked from Harlow to me. "And she will need support. She doesn't need negativity. She needs a team. You are the most important part of that team."

I swallowed against the tight grip my fear had on my throat. I needed her. Fuck this. I needed her to live. To be safe. I managed a nod. It was the best I could do.

"Hypertension is a major concern at this point. Her blood pressure should be checked morning and night. She needs to get moderate exercise. Maybe stroll down the beach for a mile but no more than that. Swimming is also good. If you have a pool, that would be ideal. Just something easy. Resting throughout the day and elevating her feet are important. She will need someone there to remind her and make sure she does this."

I nodded again. If persuading Harlow to end this pregnancy was impossible, then I intended to make sure she did all of this. If I had to quit my damn job, I would.

"Around the eighteenth week of pregnancy, we will do a fetal echocardiogram to check and see if the baby has indeed inherited the condition. We need to know this before delivery. It could save the baby's life." The doctor glanced down at his clipboard, then back up, looking first at Harlow and then at me. "I've arranged for Harlow to meet with a cardiologist bi-weekly. I've sent him her records, and we will meet to discuss Harlow before her first visit next week. It is a key factor in making this a successful pregnancy."

Harlow nodded beside me, and then her small hand slipped into mine and squeezed. She needed my reassurance, and I was standing here trying to deal with my own fear. I wasn't considering the fear that she had to be feeling. Yet she was still determined to do this.

"Be aware that you are in the high-risk category, but there are different levels within that. From what we can determine at this point, you're on the lower end of the scale. That's a good thing. A very good thing," he said, and Harlow's hand squeezed mine again. "As for intercourse, it's allowed. However, her heart is working overtime right now. Nothing too intense." He looked at me.

"But we can have, uh, sex? Right? Just nothing too, um, creative?"

The doctor bit back a grin in response to Harlow's timid question. After clearing his throat, he nodded. "Yes. Normal activity is fine. If you follow the other instructions I gave you, then there should no problem. Pregnancy normally requires more than average activity," he replied as he moved his gaze back to me. "Now, I'll see you next week after your visit with Dr. Nelson. He will fax over your results from the visit, and we will move on from there."

Harlow nodded and stood up, still holding my hand.

"Thank you," she said with such sincerity it broke my heart. She wanted this so bad. How was I supposed to oppose it? How was I supposed to convince her not to do it when she wanted it so desperately? "Let's go," she said, looking up at me.

"Thanks," I told the doctor, and walked with Harlow to the door.

A nurse met us in the hallway. "We have a back exit to take you through. That way, Miss Manning doesn't have to deal with the crowd in the waiting room."

The way she said "crowd" snapped me out of my emotional haze. What crowd?

"There have been a few arrivals since you got here. We've called the police. It should be cleared up soon," the nurse explained.

Shit. Damn Melody. Had she alerted the fucking media?

"I'm so sorry," Harlow said. I turned my attention to her and saw the horrified look on her face. Dammit. Why hadn't I been better prepared to keep her safe from this?

"Nothing to be sorry for, Miss Manning. We should have brought you in through the back. That was our mistake. From now on, you can enter through this door, and we will send you directly to an exam room. You can have your privacy then."

"Thank you," Harlow muttered, but I didn't miss the frustrated sound in her voice. She didn't like the attention, and she had flown under the radar for so long. This thing with her parents had taken her privacy away from her.

Harlow

We could have sex. As upset as I was by the media showing up at the doctor's office, it didn't take away from the fact that we could have sex. I'd been having vivid fantasies about Grant lately, and I had to fight the urge to climb on top of him when we got to the car.

"How do you feel about this doctor?" Grant asked as he pulled out of the parking lot and back onto the road toward home.

"I like him. I feel better talking to him than I did with the last doctor. This one seems to know more about my specific situation," I replied honestly. This doctor had explained things carefully and was thorough with his exam. He had even set up visits to a cardiologist for me. I had a cardiologist in L.A., but I needed one here. I needed one involved in this pregnancy. The only fear I had now was that our baby might not be healthy. I didn't want to curse this child with my heart condition.

"He seems positive," Grant said.

I liked that he seemed positive. It made me feel like I wasn't the only person on earth who believed I could do this. "I'm low-risk." I repeated the doctor's words. I liked being low-risk.

"Yeah," was all he said, although I could still see the

pinched look on his face. He wasn't going to accept things that easily. I understood that he was scared. The baby was hurting me, in his eyes. He needed to accept that the baby was a gift. I believed he would in time.

"Grant," I said, staring at his arms flexing as he drove. I wanted to lick his biceps. I was close to begging.

He glanced over at me. His eyes took me in, then went wide before he swung his gaze back to the road. "What you thinking about, baby?"

I was thinking I wanted to lick his biceps. Then his abs and that wonderful muscle that made a V and disappeared into his jeans. That was what I was thinking. "About you," I said.

"Shit," he muttered, and he took a deep breath.

"The doctor said it was OK," I reminded him.

He nodded. "Yeah, I heard him."

I reached over and ran a finger down his arms and wrapped my hand around the muscle, which flexed as he gripped the steering wheel more tightly.

"What are you doing?" he asked in a shaky voice.

I had jumped on him in a car before. But this time, I wasn't going to do that. We weren't far from his apartment. I wanted to have time to explore him and kiss every perfectly sculpted part of his body.

"Harlow?" he repeated when I didn't respond.

"I'm just touching you. I can't wait to do more," I told him as I ran my finger up over his shoulder. I brushed my fingertips over the vein in his neck, which stood out as if he were in pain.

"I can feel that, but I won't be able to drive if you keep that up."

Maybe I couldn't wait until we made it back to the apartment. "Could you pull over?" I asked, feeling my breathing pick up with anticipation.

Grant let out a string of curses before pulling off an exit and into the parking lot of the first nice hotel we came to, which we had seen from the highway. He had barely put the truck into park when he swung his door open and jumped out. I watched in fascination as he stalked around the front of the truck and opened my door.

Both of his hands grabbed my waist, and he pulled me out of the truck, even though I didn't need his help.

"Not taking you in a damn truck," was all he said as he grabbed my hand and led us inside.

It took him no time to get a room. When we stepped onto the elevator, he backed me up against the wall and kissed me. Really kissed me for the first time since he'd shown up at Mase's. This kiss wasn't holding back anything. His hands gripped my hips tightly in a possessive, hungry grasp as his mouth moved over mine. When his tongue slid across mine, I tasted the mint from his gum and shivered at the intimate contact. The dinging of the elevator reminded us that we weren't alone yet.

Grant broke the kiss and then stepped back to stare down at me. "I need to taste you. All of you," he said, before taking my hand again and leading me down the hall toward room 2200. He touched the key card to the door, and the green light blinked. He swung the door open, revealing a suite.

"We just needed a bed," I said, smiling as I looked around at the large room, complete with a bar and a gas fireplace.

"Once I get you naked, baby," he said, closing in on me, "I

don't intend to let you get dressed for a while. We need a nice big tub and a place where I can cuddle you. Not just a bed."

Oh. OK.

Grant started to lower his mouth to mine, then stopped. Suddenly, I was in the air. "We need a bed. Now," he said, pressing a kiss to my lips as he walked us toward the bedroom. He laid me down, then stood back up and stared at me. The hunger and desire were there, but the love . . . it was burning even stronger. "I'm sorry," he said, without moving to take off my clothes or his own, even though I really wanted one of us to be getting naked.

"About what?" I asked, confused.

He ran a finger down the side of my face in a gentle caress. "For hurting you. For letting you leave me. For being a son of a bitch," he whispered as he continued to gaze down at me.

I leaned up on my elbows. "You're forgiven. Now, would you get naked?" I said with a smile. He starting laughing as he reached for the hem of his shirt and pulled it over his head, gifting me with the view of his spectacular chest. Oh, yes. That was what I wanted.

"You're a little impatient, aren't you, sweet girl?" he said in a sexy drawl. He unsnapped his jeans and left them open before bending down to press a kiss to my lips. "I've never seen you so needy," he said as he nibbled on my bottom lip and took small, little licks, sending me into a frenzy.

"I told you I missed you," I reminded him, feeling a little self-conscious for being so demanding.

"Yeah, you did. I thought you missed my handsome face. Didn't know you missed the pleasure," he said in a teasing tone as his hands found the button on my jeans.

I watched his defined muscles move and flex deliciously as he tugged my jeans down and then crawled over me like a hungry lion. He stopped at my stomach and pressed a kiss just below my navel, then traveled up as he moved my T-shirt up. I lifted my arms so he could slip my shirt off. His hands made quick work of my bra, and he threw it to the floor. The sight of his large, tanned hands cupping my now-swollen breasts made me tremble.

"They're bigger," he said, holding them as if they were something precious.

"Happens during pregnancy," I explained, but I was barely able to speak above a whisper. He lowered his mouth, and his tongue darted out to lick at one of my very attentive nipples. Just the sight of him had them standing at attention. I was now so excited they tingled.

"Oh!" I gasped, twisting my hands in the covers underneath me. Grant's eyes shot up to me, and he watched me closely as he pulled my overly eager nipple into his mouth. "Ahhhh!" I cried out. There was no use trying not to make noises. I couldn't control myself.

Grant let it pop from his mouth as he ran his lips over the tip and pressed a trail of kisses to the other one, giving it the same amount of attention, as I made desperate, panting pleas.

When he started to pull away, my hands left their firm grip on the sheets to grab his hair instead and hold him there. I was so close to a release with just his mouth alone. I didn't want him leaving me now.

"Let me go lower, baby. I want to taste some more," he said in a husky whisper as he stared up at me, brushing his lips over my sensitive buds. I eased my firm hold on his ear, and he grinned before kissing back down my body. He didn't have to open my legs—I was shamelessly opening them for him. I knew where he was headed, and I wanted him there. More than anything else in the world at this moment, I wanted Grant Carter's head between my legs.

Grant

If Harlow cried out and made that whimpering, begging sound one more time, I was going to lose my shit. I swear to God, I had never been this worked up in my life. Every time I touched her, she trembled and writhed beneath me like she couldn't get enough. I felt like I had some magical touch, and it was a fucking heady feeling.

With every swipe of my tongue, she cried out my name, and her hands were back in my hair as if she had to hold on to me to keep from falling. I loved it. I loved this power and knowing she was receiving pleasure at my hands. With my mouth. Fuck, this was mind-blowing.

"Please, inside me, please," she said in a desperate pant, and I didn't let my fears or any other thought stop me. I stood up and got rid of my jeans in one move, then slid back over her. She opened her legs to me so willingly and grabbed my arms with her hands as her body arched into me. I hadn't even gotten inside her yet, and she was moaning. Holy fuck.

"Baby, you keep doing that, and I won't last very long. This will be over way too soon," I told her as I slid slowly into her. My eyes rolled back, and this time, the moan of pleasure was mine. She felt tighter and almost swollen inside. There was nothing in my life that had ever felt this good. Not even the first time I'd been inside her. This . . . this was it. The moment that changed your world. The moment that didn't just show you heaven but walked you right inside it.

"*Grant*!" she screamed as she wrapped her legs around me. Her silky heat began to squeeze me hard. She clawed at my back and chanted my name. That was all it took for me to follow her. Throwing back my head, I cried out her name and filled her. Marked her.

Made sure she would never doubt that she was mine.

❈

"Can we do it again?" Harlow asked after we both caught our breath.

Chuckling, I rolled over and pulled her over on top of me. "Not right yet. I'd rather put you in a bath and let you soak while I get us some room service. Then I intend to give you a foot massage and hold you on that big-ass sofa out there in front of the fireplace." She needed pampering. Hadn't she been listening to the doctor?

"I like foot massages . . . but I like sex better."

"No overdoing it. You heard the doctor. Let's take it easy on you, OK? Let me take care of you. Please," I said, needing her to understand.

She let out an exaggerated sigh. "Fine. I guess I'll let you bathe me and spoil me. *Sacrifices*."

Laughing, I kissed her head and moved to get up. I couldn't sit here with her in my arms like this and not get carried away.

I only needed a little encouragement. "You stay put. I'll go get your bath ready. Then I'll come get you," I told her before grabbing my jeans and tugging them back on.

She rolled over to watch me. "You could get into the bath with me," she said, with her eyes on the zipper of my jeans.

"Not that strong, baby. I'll have to settle for bathing you instead." I headed for the bathroom before I caved in and did whatever she asked me to.

"Grant," she called out after me.

"Yeah?" I turned back to see her sitting up in the bed with the sheet at her waist so that her beautiful, much larger tits were right there for me to drool over.

"I don't have to get off for us to . . . do things. I can always take care of you. I like doing that."

Grabbing the door handle before my knees buckled, I sucked in a deep breath. Holy hell. Gulping, I forced a smile. "Harlow, I'm not sure I'm strong enough for this. You're gonna drive me crazy."

She grinned and shrugged, causing her chest to bounce, capturing my undivided attention again. They were so beautiful, round, soft . . . *fuck!* I had to get away from her for a minute.

Jerking my head around, I looked into the bathroom. "Gonna run your bathwater now," I said in a strangled voice.

Harlow laughed behind me, and the musical sound almost made the fact that I already had a raging hard-on again OK. She was happy. I wanted her happy. Even if it was at my expense.

Once I had the water temperature right, I added some of the bath salts the hotel had provided and turned to get her, only to find her standing there with the sheet wrapped around her and all that dark hair in a rumpled mess. I just stood and stared at her. She was beautiful. Everything about her was beautiful. I'd known that the first time I met her. It was something you could see in her eyes. The beauty inside shone through.

But now . . . she was mine.

She was all mine.

"Sure you won't get in with me?" she asked, letting the sheet drop to the floor.

"Harlow," I said as my eyes took in her body. The small scar on her chest, which I had ignored before, jumped out at me now. In the bathroom lighting, it stood out, reminding me of everything I could lose. Of everything I would die to protect. My Harlow.

"Get into the bath and relax. Let me order you something to eat. Then I'll be back to wash your back and anything else you'll let me wash," I said as she moved toward me.

She stuck out her bottom lip. It was so unlike Harlow that I was taken aback and a little speechless. My sweet girl had become a seductress, and I wasn't sure how to deal with it. She could control me so easily. "If you insist, but I have several places I need washed," she said, brushing past me and stepping into the tub.

Fuck me. "This new Harlow isn't making things easy on me," I told her.

She glanced back over her shoulder as she sank slowly into the water. "I'm the same Harlow. I'm just secure in the man who loves me. I have nothing to hide from you."

That right there was the reason this woman owned me.

Harlow

Grant brought a tray of fruit and cheese into the bathroom, along with sparkling water. I let him feed me and tried not to tease him too badly. He was trying so hard to take care of me. If this made him feel like he was protecting me, then I would let him do it.

Once he finished bathing me and drying me off, he carried me to the living room and tucked us under a blanket on the sofa. The gas fireplace was lit, and he opened the window wide so we had a view of the Gulf.

We didn't talk much. Instead, we just watched the waves crash on the shore and the people walking up and down the beach. When someone swam out into the water, I wondered if Grant's thoughts went to Jace. I didn't know him, but even mine did. It made me sad for everyone who had lost him, especially Bethy. Now that I had Grant, I couldn't imagine what she was going through.

"We get to hear the heartbeat next week," he finally said, breaking the silence. There was a pained sound to his voice, as if he weren't sure what he thought about that.

"I know. I'm anxious," I told him, but I didn't look up at him. I couldn't right now. I was excited and hopeful, but I knew his face would portray something completely different.

"I don't want you to think that I don't want a child with you. You're the only woman on earth I want to have my baby. But I want you more. I just . . . I don't think I can do this without you. If I lost you . . ." He stopped and swallowed hard. I could hear it.

I turned in his arms and laid my head on his chest. I knew what he was saying. If I died, he didn't think he could be a father to the baby. I knew otherwise. It would take him time, but I knew he would become the world's best father. "We're going to be OK," I assured him.

His arms tightened around me, and he held me close. The beating of his heart comforted me. Closing my eyes, I embraced the moment and decided I would create a vault in my brain to keep the memories of times like this one. Maybe even write some of them down. Yes, that was what I would do: I would write moments like this one down for our baby to read one day . . . just in case.

If I wasn't around to raise the child, then I wanted our baby to know how much I loved it and that it was born out of love. Until a few months ago, I hadn't known just how much love I had been born from. Seeing Kiro with Emily had changed everything for me. I had heard that he loved my mother, but growing up and watching him treat women as if they were nothing but toys made it a little hard to believe. Then I saw him with my mother. I saw him brush her hair, heard him talk to her so sweetly. She couldn't talk back—she didn't even know he was there—but he adored her. Even now. After all this time.

I wish I had known that as a child. It would have given me more security and trust. I wanted our child never to question that Grant and I loved each other.

But now wasn't the time to tell Grant about my idea to write notes to the baby. He didn't need reminders of the future. I believed I was strong enough to make it. I wanted him to believe that, too.

"Rush said that your dad doesn't know about the pregnancy," Grant said, threading his fingers through mine.

I hadn't told Dad, because I knew he would be furious that I was going through with it. He had enough to deal with right now, protecting Emily from the world. Slacker Demon was no longer touring, and everything had changed for him in a few short months.

"I don't think he needs anything else to deal with right now. He has his hands full," I explained.

"He's gonna find out. The doctor's office today . . ." He trailed off.

I hadn't thought about that. Would the media mention that I was visiting an ob-gyn? Would they say something about Grant being with me? Oh, crap. "Do you think they'll even mention that? They didn't get a photo of either of us."

Grant let out a sigh and squeezed my hand. "Yeah, baby. I think they will. Right now, you're hard to get any info on, and they've been trying. With your dad off the grid, they're searching for anything. And they don't necessarily need evidence to stir up some drama."

I would have to call my dad. He couldn't find out this way.

"I'll call him tomorrow when we get home. Actually, are we going home today or tomorrow?" I asked, looking around the suite he had booked just so we could have sex. Did he intend for us to stay here tonight?

"I want you in my bed," he said as he brushed his thumb over my bottom lip.

I wanted to be in his bed, too. I wanted to get back to Rosemary Beach, and I wanted to be with him. Seeing Blaire was a plus. There were things about pregnancy that I wanted to ask her about. And I wanted to see Nate.

"You ready to go?" I asked him.

A cocky grin touched his sexy lips. "Yeah, but first, I want something to eat."

We had just eaten. I frowned, and Grant's sexy grin stayed in place as he laid me back on the sofa. He leaned down over me and brushed his lips against mine. "I wasn't talking about food," he whispered.

I managed to grab onto the sofa and hold on tight while he moved down my body and began to love me with his very talented mouth.

"Ah! OK . . . you can't . . . do this . . . Ah! Oh, God! But I get to do the same to you next." I panted as his tongue circled my clit. He lifted his head to look up at me. Seeing his beautiful mouth right there, hovering over me, made me tremble. It was a breathtaking sight.

"You don't have to bargain with me to get me to let you put that sexy mouth on me," he said. He kept his eyes on me as he flicked his tongue over my swollen, aching bud. "Tastes so damn good. I missed this." He placed both of his hands on my thighs and pushed them open farther. "Could eat this all fucking day and never get tired of it."

His naughty words had me crying out things I wasn't sure made sense. I was lost to the sensation. Nothing mattered at the moment but him. And this.

Grant

I had been woken up by two texts and a call from the job site in Sandestin. We had a condo going up there, and they had some issues I had to handle. Leaving Harlow curled up in my big bed like an angel wasn't easy.

She had been asleep when we got home last night, and I'd carried her to bed and undressed her. All she had managed was a few mumbled sentences that didn't make sense, but they'd been damn cute.

I fixed my thermos of coffee and swept up the mud that had piled up by the door, because I really didn't want Harlow seeing that. I'd have to get someone else to come in and clean the rest of the place today. Glancing at my phone, I knew I needed to go, but I was waiting for Rush to wake up Blaire and get her to call me. If I had to leave Harlow, I wanted someone keeping her company today.

The screen lit up, and I sighed in relief at Blaire's name.

"Hey," I said, walking away from the bedroom door so I wouldn't wake Harlow.

"Good morning. You're back?" Blaire asked.

"*We're* back," I replied. "She needs sleep, but she'll want to see you and needs a friend while I'm gone. I won't be but a few hours. I wouldn't normally go, but it's a big client, and I need to fix some shit."

"I'm dressing now. Rush is going to spend the day with Nate, and I'll take care of Harlow. Don't worry about her. I won't leave her."

I didn't have a sister, but Blaire was a damn good alternative. "Thank you so much."

"You're welcome, but this is for me as much as you. I want to see her. You weren't the only one who missed her."

Smiling, I grabbed my keys and made sure to leave the note on the counter where she would see it. "Yeah, but I missed her the most."

Blaire chuckled. "I won't argue with that."

"Thanks again, Blaire. I left her a note to call you when she gets up. But she may not call. I never know with her. She worries about bothering people."

"I'll just show up in an hour or so. Go to work, Grant. I got this."

"Yes, ma'am." I hung up and stuck my phone into my pocket. Glancing back at the bedroom door, I saw it open slowly. Harlow walked out, dressed in one of my T-shirts, which I had put on her last night. Her hair was all over the place, and her face had pillow creases on it. I had never seen anything more beautiful.

"You leaving?" she asked in a sleepy voice.

I walked back to her. "I didn't want to wake you. I've got an issue at one of the job sites," I explained as I slid my arms around her waist.

"OK. I heard you talking," she said, blinking slowly while her eyes adjusted to the sunlight pouring into the room.

"I called Blaire. She's coming to keep you company today. She missed you."

A smile lit up her face. "Oh, good. I wanted to see her."

Leaving sucked, but this made it a little easier. I was giving her space to be alone and have girl time. Harlow had very little of that in her life, and I wanted her to have good friendships. The girl I'd first met didn't have anyone. She lived for her books and stayed in her room. I wanted more for Harlow than that.

"I'll be back as soon as I can. You enjoy your time with Blaire, but call me if you need anything." I kissed her lips. Nothing was ever as good as kissing Harlow.

She wrapped her arms around my neck and melted into me. This didn't make leaving easier. I was about ready to say screw the job site when she stepped back and pressed a hand to her now-swollen lips. "OK, go. We can do that when you get back."

"You be ready for me, because I have plans for you when I get home," I told her, then blew her a kiss before finally leaving. I was going to be a little late, but they could wait. I'd get there when I got there.

To my precious baby,

The day I first saw him, my knees went a little weak, and my stomach fluttered. Like that feeling of butterflies taking off. That was how I felt when I laid eyes on your dad for the first time. He was beautiful. I had never considered a man beautiful before, but Grant Carter was beautiful.

I never imagined he would notice me. I was quiet and introverted. I didn't make friends easily, and I didn't trust others. Those are things I never want you to experience or feel. I've overcome them because I've found your father.

That night, he cornered me and sent my tiny infatuation into a full-blown crush with only a few words. But I was terrified. Completely scared out of my wits. I wasn't used to dealing with men when they flirted with me. I didn't know then that he would change my life.

I also didn't know that life was full of color and excitement. I had hidden away and remained alone for so long. I was missing out on so much. But your dad taught me to live. He taught me about love, and he gave me the greatest gift anyone could ever give me: you.

When you are old enough to read this letter, I hope I'm sitting there beside you. I hope I'm the one who gets to read it to you. But if I'm not there physically, know that I am there with you in spirit. Always. I will never leave your side. And I will love you forever.

You were created from a love so strong, a love that should be grown and shared.

And now we have you to share it with.

Love you always,
Mommy

Harlow

I didn't have friends until Blaire. She was engaged to Rush Finlay when I met her, and I immediately liked her, because there was a kindness in her eyes. Also, if someone could make Rush fall in love with her, she had to be special. He used to be one of the most cynical people I knew . . . until he met Blaire. And now they had their son, Nate. Rush was a totally different person now.

Having Blaire to talk to was wonderful, but walking into Kerrington Country Club wasn't something I wanted to do just yet. Blaire had casually mentioned that my evil half sister was in Paris right now, but I was still on edge. I didn't want to see Nan. Ever again, if possible.

Grant had been with Nan once. Forgetting that was easier now. He loved me; I knew that, and I was secure in that. But still, Nan was the kind of beautiful that I couldn't compete with. I had hidden from the Nans of the world until my dad had sent me to live with her while he went on tour.

"You look like you want to throw up. Are you OK?" Blaire asked as I walked beside her toward the entrance to the restaurant at the club where we'd be having breakfast this morning.

"I'm fine," I assured her.

The door opened, and we were greeted by a guy dressed in the typical uniform of slacks and a polo with the Kerrington Club monogram on it.

"Good morning, Mrs. Finlay, Miss Manning," the guy said with a polite smile.

"Morning, Clint. Is Jimmy working the morning shift?" Blaire asked.

The guy's grin got bigger, almost as if hearing Jimmy's name made him happy. "Yes, he is."

Blaire chuckled softly and thanked him, then we walked to the hostess.

"Two, Mrs. Finlay?" the girl asked, her eyes quickly darting away from me as if she was trying not to stare but wanted to be sure she was seeing me. I hated this sudden fame that came with my dad.

"Please, and we'd like to sit in Jimmy's section," she replied.

The girl nodded, still staring at me with wide eyes. Crap, this could not be good.

"And"—Blaire paused and looked at the girl's name badge—"April, if media of any kind were to show up at the club, Mr. Kerrington would be very upset. I'll be sending him and Della a text once we're seated asking them to up the security. Do you understand what I am telling you?" Blaire was a badass. I wanted to be like her.

The girl bobbed her head and swallowed nervously. "Yes, Mrs. Finlay, of course."

Blaire beamed a smile at the girl. "Thank you, April. I appreciate your help."

April blushed as if Blaire had just paid her a high compliment, then led us to our seats. I don't think the girl wanted to leave our table; I was almost prepared for her to ask for an autograph.

"All right, April, stop your fangirling, and let these women breathe. They came for breakfast, not to be gawked at. Damn, girl," Jimmy said as he walked up to our table.

Poor April scampered away.

"She's new, but she's sweet. I can work with that," Jimmy said, then blasted a smile our way. "Look at you two gorgeous women without your overprotective men, eating here alone. I might take advantage and make my move."

Blaire's eyebrows rose, and she looked knowingly at Jimmy. "I think Clint might get a little upset if you did that, hmm?"

Jimmy laughed and shot her a wink. "You picked up on that one fast."

"He was all smiles when I asked if you were here. I'd have to be blind not to pick up on it."

Jimmy smirked. He knew he was beautiful, but he was one of the nicest people I'd met here in Rosemary Beach. "What can I get you two to drink? Coffee, maybe? Or cappuccinos?"

I had strict instructions to stay away from caffeine. "I'll take an orange juice," I told him.

"I'd love a cappuccino, thanks, Jimmy," Blaire said, and glanced down at her menu.

I wondered if she even had to look at the menu. She had worked here until Rush had demanded she stop when she got pregnant. I assumed she knew the menu by heart at this point.

"The quiche is great, but then, so are the raspberry and cheese scones," Blaire told me.

I decided quiche with a whole-wheat croissant would do. I was trying not to eat sugar—it was healthier for me to avoid it.

"Uh-oh, he looks like he's on a mission," Blaire said in a whisper, and I looked up to see Woods Kerrington taking long strides toward us. He looked concerned. He stopped at our table and turned his attention to me. Those dark eyes of his were serious, but Blaire was right: he meant business.

"Kiro just got past security. They said he was cursing and ranting about finding you. I've called Rush, and he said to get the two of you to my office and lock you up until he deals with Kiro. The guys working security said he was furious and has been drinking."

My dad was here. He knew. That was the only excuse for him acting this way. Blaire immediately stood up and reached for her purse. "Come on, let's get you out of here."

"I need to be here," Woods said. "He has a driver, but I don't think he's prepared to deal with him. Kiro's liable to knock my valet guys out if they say the wrong thing to him."

"I'll get her to your office," Blaire assured Woods, and she grabbed my arm. "Come on, I know a back way."

I didn't have to run from my dad. I had never run from him in the past. I wasn't scared of his angry ranting. He never got mad at me. But if he thought the baby was harming me, he wouldn't be happy. He wasn't used to being told no, and this time, I would be telling him no.

"Do you think you can calm him down? Or maybe Rush can?" I asked Woods.

Woods nodded. "Finlay can handle him. You get out of here."

I did what he said and ran from my dad. I felt horribly guilty about it. It worried me that he was drinking again. Was Emily OK? Had something happened with her? Did he need me? Maybe he didn't know about the baby. Maybe he was just having a wild, drunken episode and missed me. It wasn't like he hadn't shown up in North Carolina like this when I was growing up. Whenever Kiro Manning missed me, he jumped on a plane and came to see me, even if it was after a concert and he was high as a kite. My grandmama had hated it when he showed up like that. The one time he had come to my school, still drunk from the night before, basking in his fame, had been humiliating. But he was my dad. I dealt with it.

"Where is she, and where is that stupid fuck who knocked her up!" Kiro's voice was slurred, but it carried down the hall as he entered the restaurant. I cringed and said a silent prayer of thanks that Grant wasn't around for this.

I couldn't hear what Woods was saying, but his voice had a hard edge.

"Rush will be here any minute," Blaire whispered as she led me into an elevator that would take us to the top floor.

I couldn't look at her. This was humiliating. She and I hadn't actually discussed my pregnancy yet or the complications. All she had said was congratulations when she had arrived this morning at Grant's condo.

When we were safely inside Woods's office, Blaire locked the door behind her and let out a sigh. "Wow, he's upset. Did you just tell him?" she asked, turning to look at me.

I walked over to the plush leather sofa, sank down into it, and dropped my head into my hands. I shouldn't be up here. I should be down there dealing with him. He wasn't going to calm down until he saw me. I just couldn't face him yet. I didn't want to hear him tell me to abort my baby.

"No. I think there were media people at the doctor's office yesterday. Paparazzi, perhaps. Not sure. They snuck us out the back."

Blaire walked over and sat down beside me. Her hand rested on my back. "It's in all the gossip news. Your 'visit to the ob-gyn with boyfriend Grant Carter.' They had some woman outside the office saying she knew Grant and was positive it was you in there."

I let out a frustrated groan. I was afraid that would happen. Stupid woman had to recognize me. "I should go talk to him."

"No. Absolutely not. You aren't dealing with him like this. Rush can get him back to our place and let him sleep it off. When he's sober, Rush can bring him over to see you, but Grant will be with you when that happens."

Blaire sounded like a mother. I would have smiled if I could manage it. Knowing my dad was downstairs, yelling my private business to the entire club, had me on the verge of tears.

My phone started ringing, and Blaire reached for my purse and pulled it out. After checking it, she handed it to me. "It's Grant," she said.

My heart ached. I wanted him here so badly. "Hello," I said, my voice cracking, tears filling my eyes.

"I'm on my way. Rush has Kiro in his car, and he's taking him to his house. Woods will be up to get you in a minute. He'll drive you home. Blaire can stay with you until I get there. Are you OK?"

I nodded and sniffled, then realized he couldn't see me nod. "Yeah, I think." I replied.

"No, you're not. Shit. I shouldn't have left you," he said, and I heard him curse and hit something. "I'm on my way, baby. I'm on my way. Be strong for me, OK?"

"I will," I assured him. "Drive safe."

"Always."

Grant

Fucking Kiro. If the man wasn't Harlow's father, I'd bury my fist in his stupid-ass face. He'd come barreling into the club and upset her. Drunk motherfucker didn't even think about how it would affect Harlow.

It took me half the time to get home than it normally did. I ran three stoplights and broke every speed limit, but I was here now. Slamming the car door behind me, I took off running up the stairs to my apartment. Harlow didn't need to get upset. She needed to be calm and happy.

I opened the front door and headed toward the voices. Blaire was fixing two glasses of water, and Harlow was siting on the sofa with her legs curled up under her. When she saw me, her eyes went wide with relief. I closed the space between us with three long strides and pulled her up into my arms.

"I'm here. You're OK."

And then she began to sob.

I was going to kill Kiro Manning.

I ran my hand over her head and whispered sweet words to her, reassuring her that I was here and it was fine. I begged her not to cry, but she clung to me, and her tears soaked my shirt. Again, I was helpless. I wasn't sure why she was crying so pitifully, but I knew it had to do with her dad, and that was enough to put him on my shit list.

"This isn't good for you," I reminded her. I couldn't say it wasn't good for the baby, because I honestly couldn't bring myself to care about anything other than Harlow's health.

"Or the baby," Blaire said, walking up behind us. I looked at her over Harlow's head, and she stared pointedly at me, scolding me for the thoughts she seemed to know I was thinking. "Drink the water, and take some deep breaths," Blaire said as she touched Harlow's arm.

Harlow sniffed and hiccupped, but she stopped sobbing and reached for the glass of water. Blaire had said the magic words. At this point, I didn't care what those magic words were, I was just thankful she was calming down.

"I'm sorry," she whispered, and took a small sip of the water. Her eyes were red and swollen, and her face was blotchy and wet.

"No, don't apologize. I just want you calm," I told her. I kept my arm around her and caressed the skin on her bare arm and shoulder, trying to soothe her.

"I just ran from him. I never run from my dad, but I just ran and hid. He must think . . . I don't know what he thinks. I just wasn't ready to face him about this."

She knew he would want her to have an abortion. Telling her dad no was going to be difficult. She loved that man. I wasn't sure why, because he was the shittiest father on the face of the earth, even though he had sweet Harlow for a daughter. All I could figure was that Emily Manning must have been an amazing woman for Harlow to overcome inheriting that man's genes.

God knew Nan got all his bad traits, along with Georgianna's.

"You needed to let him sober up. You did the right thing," Blaire assured her.

Harlow sipped her water as she stared straight ahead at nothing. I hated seeing her like this, but facing her dad wasn't something I could stop her from doing. Kiro was above the law. He had proved that with his latest mishaps. No one wanted to press charges.

"When he wakes up, I want to see him. I won't feel better until I've seen him," she said in a whisper, not looking at Blaire or me but still straight ahead.

"Rush is going to call the second he thinks Kiro is ready to come over here," I told her. I had spoken to Rush on my way back home. He had been dealing with Kiro, but he'd promised to let me know the minute he'd sobered him up. Bethy had come over to take care of Nate. I knew it was only a matter of time before Blaire left to get Nate.

"He's going to demand I get an abortion," Harlow said, finally turning her gaze up at me.

I couldn't tell her that he wouldn't. I had no doubt that he'd all but throw her into his limo in an attempt to get her to the best abortion clinic in L.A. I realized he wanted what I wanted, but the difference was that I refused to let him force her to do anything.

"Why don't you rest? Let Grant hold you and try not to think about it. Just remember, the baby needs you to stay calm. And Grant needs you to be OK," Blaire told her. "I'm going to get Nate from Bethy. It'll be his nap time soon, and Bethy won't be able to get him to sleep."

Harlow nodded and stepped away from me to hug Blaire. "Thank you for everything. I'm sorry our day got messed up."

"I'm sorry, too, but we'll make it up. You worry about taking care of you and the baby right now. Let Grant take care of you." Blaire's words were gentle but firm. She seemed to know how to talk to Harlow.

"Thanks," I told her.

She smiled and patted my arm. "You got this. It's going to be OK," she said softly before leaving.

When the door closed behind Blaire, Harlow turned to me and let out a weary sigh. "I think I want a nap, too."

Good. She needed to rest. "Come on, sweet girl. We'll get you into bed, and I'll even let you use me as your pillow."

A small smile tugged on her sad face. "That's a deal any girl would have a hard time turning down."

I slipped my arm around her shoulder. "Yeah, but you're the only girl I'd offer my chest as a pillow to."

"Lucky me," she said in a teasing voice.

"No, lucky me," I replied.

⌗

My ringing phone woke me up hours later. I eased out from under Harlow and silenced it until I could get out of the room. Glancing down, I saw my dad's name. He was pissed. I hadn't seen the work problem through today, and he was probably just now hearing how I'd run out of there with no explanation.

"Hello," I said, preparing to hear him yell at me.

"Is it true?" he asked, and I glanced back down at my phone to make sure I had read the caller's name correctly. I had. This was my father.

"What are you talking about?" I asked, confused.

"Did you get Kiro Manning's daughter knocked up? The one with the heart condition?"

Shit. When did my dad start listening to celebrity gossip news?

"Don't call her knocked up. I'm in love with her. This wasn't some cheap fling. We were in a committed relationship when this happened."

He was silent a moment, then let out a groan of frustration. "Son, if the news is right, she has a congenital heart defect. Having a baby isn't recommended. It could be fatal."

Did he think we didn't know that? I wasn't an idiot. "I know that," I replied through clenched teeth.

"And Kiro Manning's daughter? Really? Have you learned nothing from watching that crowd and hanging out with Rush?" My dad was once married to Rush's mother, Georgianna. I was a little kid when they were married, and it was a short marriage. He wasn't a fan of anyone connected to them.

"She's nothing like them. She's . . . wonderful, Dad. She's too damn good for me, but she loves me."

"Her heart—"

"I know about her heart! Dammit, I understand what could happen. I don't want her to have this baby. I want to save her, but she's determined. She loves this baby so much already, and she refuses to listen to anyone tell her she can't bring it into this world. And I love her too much to walk away just to save my heart from being destroyed. I can't leave her, so if this is what she wants, I will take this chance and ride this ride and pray like hell I don't lose her."

Dad didn't say anything for a few minutes. "I've never loved a woman like that. But I'm glad you found it. Just be careful. Call me if you need me. And get your ass back to Sandestin tomorrow and straighten out that order."

"Yes, sir," I replied.

"'Bye," he said, then he was gone. Call ended.

He never said he loved me, and he never got very deep with me. Our relationship was based on business. I often wondered if he'd even call me at all if I didn't work for him, so I was stunned by our conversation. This was the first time he'd admitted to not loving my mom. I always thought he had. I thought she'd ruined him. She was a beautiful, selfish, ambitious woman who traded up for husbands with more money on a regular basis. Sometimes she settled for sugar daddies to keep her in luxurious surroundings. The last time I had spoken to my mom, she'd been . . . hell, I wasn't even sure where she lived now. It had been that long.

I set my phone down and headed back to the bedroom. I wondered if my dad would ever ask about Harlow and the baby again.

To my precious baby,

You came into this world with something special that many kids aren't blessed with: a wonderful father. I know that by the time you read this letter, you will know just how amazing your dad is. To be loved by him is to live. And I lived because he loved me.

You have his love now, too. We may be sharing it together. If we are, then we're the two luckiest people on earth.

My experience with my own daddy was more complicated. He was just a different kind of daddy. He loved me, which I never doubted, but he's unique, as I'm sure you already know. Being Kiro Manning's grandchild would be interesting, I imagine. I hope you won't be the only one for long. Uncle Mase will have kids one day, and I know you'll have a close relationship with them.

Your grandfather might do things that make you question him, but when you're having mixed feelings about him, know that I love him. He was my world for a very long time. He became a different man once he lost your grandmother, and he has never been the same since. It changed him. So, love him anyway. Even when he's crazy, love him. Love him because I love him. Because he loves me and because he won't be able to help but love you.

I hope one day, we can curl up in your bed together

and giggle about something he said or did. He's an unforgettable character, and he will love you. I know he will.

Love you always,
Mommy

Harlow

My eyes opened, and I was in bed alone. My Grant pillow was gone, but I was tucked in, and the pillow Grant had slept on was still warm. Then I heard him.

My dad was here.

Grant was talking, but I couldn't hear what he was saying. I sat up and took several deep breaths. I had to stay calm. Getting upset wasn't good for the baby. I had to protect the baby. And I had to protect myself. Standing up, I ran my hand through my hair and looked at myself in the mirror. My eyes were still slightly swollen from earlier, but I looked rested.

Kiro started raising his voice, and I knew Grant needed me to rescue him. My dad was in a foul mood. I had to remember he was just scared. He'd already lost so much in life.

The room fell silent when I opened the door, and both men turned to look at me. I gave Grant a reassuring smile before turning my attention to Kiro. He looked awful. He had lost weight since I'd seen him last, and there were dark circles under his eyes. He wasn't wearing any jewelry. If he weren't covered in tattoos, he'd look like an average older man. But he was a rock god. The world's rock god. My dad.

"Hey, Daddy," I said, breaking the silence that had fallen over the room.

Pain contorted his face, and he shook his head. "You can't do this, baby girl. I won't let you. I need you. Gambling with your life sure as hell ain't gonna fly. I'm taking you to get this fixed."

"No," I interrupted him. I had known what he would say, but hearing him actually say it was too hard. "No," I repeated for emphasis. "I'm staying here. I have an obstetrician who specializes in pregnancies like mine. He's teamed up with a cardiologist, and I will see him weekly. Yes, this is a high-risk pregnancy compared with normal ones, but I'm considered low-risk in my category. The doctor is positive about this."

"But there's still a risk. Why? Why would you do this to me? You know I need you. This—this . . . thing isn't even a baby yet. It's just a fetus. It can kill you, Harlow. I can't allow anything to take you away from me. Your mother wouldn't want this. Emmy would be heartbroken. Is this a religious thing? Is this some shit your grandmama taught you? Because it's bullshit! Do you hear me! *Bullshit.*"

"*Daddy!* Stop. I want this baby. It's our baby. Mine and Grant's. I love this baby—and it *is* a baby, not a thing. It's *our* baby, and I love it so much." My voice broke, and Grant was beside me in an instant, his arm wrapping around my shoulders.

Kiro shifted his gaze from me to Grant, and a furious gleam lit his eyes. "This is your fault," he said.

"Daddy, no— "

"If she dies, I will kill you. Do you understand me, boy? I will end you."

"Daddy, stop—"

"She's all I've got. You can make babies with some woman who won't get killed by it. You didn't have to knock up my baby girl—the only fucking thing I have left of Emmy." Kiro shook his head. "You don't know what it's like to love someone like I love Emmy. You have no fucking clue. And Harlow is part of Emmy. My Emmy."

My stomach felt sick, and my chest hurt. I hated hearing him talk about Emily, my mother. He still grieved over the life he had lost with her. It broke my heart over and over again now that I knew the truth behind my father's rock-and-roll image.

"Harlow is my world. I love her, and I will do anything to protect her. She's my *only* concern. But she also wants this baby. I won't force her to do something she doesn't want to do." Grant's words sounded grave and tense.

Kiro continued to glare at him. "Really? Because you sure weren't thinking about keeping her safe when you fucked her without protection," he snarled.

Grant flinched.

"Daddy, please stop this."

"I didn't know about her heart. I never would've . . ." Grant swallowed and took a deep, ragged breath. "Never would've done anything to hurt her. I had no idea she had this condition. I wasn't trying to get her pregnant."

"But you did," Kiro said in a hateful tone. Then he turned his attention back to me. "You've always known you couldn't have kids, Harlow. It wasn't something we kept from you. I warned you all your life that you had to be careful and take care of yourself, that your heart wasn't as strong as others'."

I had lived in fear as a child because Kiro had convinced me that if I did anything exciting, my heart would stop working. I didn't understand what was wrong with it, but I knew it was broken. I hated being broken. "I don't want to live like I'm broken. I'm strong, Daddy. I've proved that over the years. I need you to believe me. Trust me that I can do this, because I'm going to. Grant can't change my mind, you can't change my mind, and no doctor can change my mind. I want this baby. I want our baby," I said, reaching for Grant's hand and threading my fingers through his.

Kiro threw up his hands and let out a string of curses, then pointed at our clasped hands. "Enjoy that, because you're killing her!" he yelled at Grant. "Life without the love of the woman who owns you makes it one empty fucking nightmare. Prepare yourself, because I've already lived this hell. I know what it's like." He took a step toward me and cupped my face in his hands. "I love you. You're my girl. Always have been," Kiro whispered, and he pressed a kiss to my cheek. Then he turned and walked out the door without another word.

I waited for it to sink in that he was gone. He was angry, but he was leaving. I would miss him, but I knew that once I survived this, he'd come around. He would be a part of our baby's life, and he would love his grandchild. I just had to live for all of us.

Grant tugged my hand until I was pressed against his chest. His body was tense, and I knew the words my dad had spat at him were going to haunt him. Kiro didn't know he had just thrown all of Grant's fears in his face.

"I'm going to be OK. I can do this," I told him with a fierceness that left little doubt. I was strong. I was going to show them all just how strong I was.

"You have to be. I can't . . . I can't live without you," he said, his voice thick with emotion.

It was my turn to reassure him. I reached up and pulled his face down to mine so I could press my lips firmly against his. He opened for me immediately, and his hands wrapped around me as he kissed me with all the love, passion, and warmth that embodied Grant Carter.

Grant

Blaire rescheduled her girls' day with Harlow and invited Della along for lunch and a trip to the spa. The idea of Harlow getting pampered made me happy. As long as the people touching her were women. Blaire had assured me they would be, then laughed at me.

I had handled the issue in Sandestin and didn't have to work, but I knew Harlow needed time with friends. I wanted to give her space. Then Woods called and asked if Rush and I wanted to join him for a round of golf. It had been a while since we'd done this. I knew the absence of Jace would be on all of our minds.

I had stepped out of the truck and reached for my clubs in the back when I smelled a familiar perfume. Shit. No one had told me Nan was back in town. I hauled the bag out of the truck bed, then turned to face Nan. My biggest mistake.

"You look better than the last time I saw you," she said with a smirk.

"I am better. You enjoy Paris?" I asked, pulling the strap of my bag up my shoulder.

"I always enjoy Paris," she said as she took a step toward me and ran her hand up my chest. "I miss you. I miss the

106

things you can do with that mouth of yours." She ran her finger over my lips.

I shook my head and started to step back, but I wasn't fast enough. Nan slipped her hand into my hair and grabbed a handful, then pressed her mouth against mine. I was in shock at first but only for a second, before I shoved her back, breaking the kiss.

"What the fuck?" I asked, furious. "You don't get to do that shit. I'm not available, and if I was, I sure as hell wouldn't be available for you."

Nan glared at me. "Not available? Don't tell me Harlow came back," she said hatefully. As if "Harlow" was a bad word that she hated saying.

"Harlow is back, and she's pregnant. *With my baby*," I said with emphasis.

Nan frowned at me. "Pregnant?" she repeated.

I nodded, a little confused at the pride that came with that word. I hated that she was pregnant. I hated that she was in danger. But there was pride in saying a part of me was inside Harlow.

"She can't get pregnant," Nan said slowly. "She has a heart condition. What the hell were you thinking?" Of all the people in the world, I expected to blame myself and scold myself for this; I never expected it from Nan. "She can't have a baby," Nan repeated, as if she wasn't sure it had sunk in for me yet.

"She's having the baby. I've tried talking her out of it, but she refuses to listen to me. She won't . . . she already loves the baby," I explained, not missing that it was slightly odd to be explaining myself to Nan.

Nan put her hand on her hip and studied me a moment

before saying anything else. "So you're just gonna let her have a baby that will kill her? Does Kiro know?"

"He was here two days ago. You just missed him."

Nan rolled her eyes. She wasn't a fan of her father's. He had neglected her for most of her life and hardly claimed her as a daughter, all while he had loved and cherished Harlow. Nan held a lot of bitterness toward both of them. "Hate that I missed that," she said sarcastically.

"I gotta go. Rush and Woods are waiting for me," I said, turning to leave her there. I didn't want to chat with Nan any longer. It was weird, and I felt like I was cheating on Harlow by just carrying on a conversation with Nan.

"Can I join?" Nan asked.

"No, you can't." Blaire's voice surprised me, and I turned around to see her walking toward us as Harlow and Della stood at the main entrance of the club. Harlow looked like she was on the verge of tears, and the pain in her eyes had me dropping my bag and heading for her.

"I don't recall asking you, Blaire," Nan snapped.

"You didn't ask me. But I'm answering," Blaire retorted. I didn't stay there to referee. They might be related by marriage now, but those two hadn't made any sort of bond. I doubted they ever would.

Della was glaring at me as I ran up the stairs to where she and Harlow were standing.

"Your car's here, Miss Sloane," the valet said as I approached.

"Not ready for it just yet. Give us a minute, please," Della replied, and she swung her angry gaze back to me.

I studied Harlow's face and saw her drop her eyes to stare at the ground. Something was wrong. Della was ready to hit me, and Harlow looked ready to sob.

"Baby, what's wrong?" I asked, touching her face in an attempt to get her to look at me.

Harlow lifted her face, but she kept her eyes diverted from me.

"Maybe you should ask Nan's lips?" Della snapped at me.

Oh. Shit! "You saw that?" I asked Harlow in a panic, and realized it wasn't the smartest reaction.

"Yes, the entire club saw it from the dining room," Della answered for her. "We were just leaving."

Not good. Upsetting Harlow was the last thing I wanted to do. "I shoved her off. I wasn't expecting her to do that. I was telling her I was going to play golf, and she just attacked me. I didn't know—"

"You kept talking to her. You didn't look angry," Harlow's soft voice finally said, interrupting my excuses.

Shit. "I told her about the baby, and she was surprised. She knows about your heart. We were discussing Kiro's visit. And your health. I swear, we were. I know that sounds crazy, but she was actually curious. And seemed concerned, which I'm having a hard time believing, too."

Harlow's eyes finally lifted to look at me, then she glanced over at Della. "OK. I'm gonna go to the spa with Blaire and Della. We can talk about it later."

She was still upset. Damn, I didn't want her leaving me while she was upset. "Come home with me. We can talk. I don't like seeing you upset. I swear to you, I didn't kiss her. She startled me, and it took me a second to react. I feel nothing for her. Nothing, Harlow. You're all I love. You."

Harlow studied my face, then nodded. "It was hard to watch," she said.

She could have put a knife in my gut, and it would have hurt less. *Dammit, Nan.* She did this shit to cause problems. I wished she'd kept her ass in Paris.

"You shouldn't have had to see that. I should have been prepared for her to try something like that and guarded against it. I thought after the last time I spoke to her, she had gotten the message that I'm not interested. That I'm completely taken."

Harlow gave me a small smile. "We have to go. I'll see you later. Have fun playing golf with the boys," she said, sounding less hurt and more relieved.

I bent my head to kiss her, and she turned her face so that my lips hit her cheek. She stepped back and ducked her head. "Sorry, but she's still on your lips. I can see her lip gloss. I can't . . ." she said, then walked down the stairs with Della right behind her. Blaire was standing at the car and pressed her hand to her mouth to cover a laugh.

I shot an annoyed look at Blaire, and she shrugged, then laughed again before getting into the car. Harlow glanced back at me as she climbed into the car and gave me a small wave. Then the valet closed the door, and they were gone.

Motherfucker.

To my precious baby,

You have so many people in your life who love you. I imagine that you love spending time with Nate by now. He'll be someone you can look up to, and he'll be like family for you. Rush was always like my family. Growing up with rock-star fathers isn't easy, and Rush and I shared that bond.

I hope that you call them Uncle Rush and Aunt Blaire. I know that they're going to welcome you with open arms. I can't think of two better people to ask to be your godparents.

Then there are Woods and Della. They're special friends, the kind of people I never expected to meet, but once again, they're a gift your father gave to me. He gave me so many. I expect Woods and Della will have kids by now and that you'll be friends with the Kerrington clan. When I was pregnant with you, Woods and Della stepped in and helped me out more than once. I cherish their friendship.

We've talked about your uncle Mase. He is going to be special in your life. Once he sees you for the first time, you'll win his heart. I know him too well. He's a big softie. Be sure to hug him often and tell him how much you love him for me. Even if I'm there with you, he will eat it up. He likes attention.

His mother, your aunt Maryann, was your first champion. She was ready to slay dragons for you, if that was what was required. Know that if you ever need anything and aren't sure who to turn to, you can go to her. She's wise and full of good advice.

Then there's your aunt Nan. I don't even know if you'll refer to her as Aunt or not. I'm not sure if she'll be in your life much or at all. I hope she is. I'm surprising myself by saying this, but I do hope you have a relationship with her. I think she has suffered from rejection so many times in her life by people who were supposed to love her unconditionally that she became bitter. It marked her. I want her to find happiness and a way to heal. Maybe we will both see that day happen. I hope we do.

So you see, you already have a family. People who are ready to meet you and love you and be there for you throughout life. You'll never be alone. It's the one thing that gives me the most comfort when I lie down to sleep at night.

Love you always,
Mommy

Harlow

The sight of Nan's hands in Grant's hair as she kissed him was tormenting me. Della and Blaire had spent the past several hours trying to get my mind off of it, so I pretended I was over it, but I wasn't. All I could think was that Nan was healthy. She'd be able to give him babies with no cause for fear. Healthy babies. She would be here if I wasn't.

The idea that Grant could love someone else someday hurt so much, but then the selfishness of that emotion made me furious with myself. If something happened to me, I wanted Grant to find happiness again. I wanted someone to love him and give him the life he deserved. I did.

Just not with Nan.

God, how wrong was that? What had happened to me? I was a nice person. I had always been a nice person, but now . . . ugh. I was disgusted with myself. I didn't know what I felt. My emotions were all over the place. I was weepy all the time and clingy. I wasn't a clingy, weepy person.

"He's already home. I bet he's been pacing and worrying his head off," Blaire said with a smile. "Don't be too hard on him. I believe Nan really did attack him. He'll learn to keep his distance."

I nodded. She was right. I knew she was, and now the idea of him being worried all day made me feel even worse. "I probably shouldn't have been so hard on him," I said.

"Yeah, you should have. He gets away with too much because he's so charming. He needed to be reminded that he can't let that kind of thing happen. If you don't let him know it bothers you, it could happen again with someone else," Blaire explained.

I trusted her. She loved Rush, but she had dealt with her own Nan battles. Nan was Rush's baby sister and had grown up with him in their mother's, Georgianna's, house. Rush had spent most of his life babying Nan and taking care of her. When Blaire walked into his life, Nan hadn't dealt well with that.

"Thanks for today. I really enjoyed it," I told them.

"I'm glad we got to do it. I missed you," Della said. Her smile was always so sincere and kind.

"We'll do it again," Blaire assured us both. "Next time, though, I'm forcing Bethy to come with us. Kicking and screaming, if I have to." Blaire had begged Bethy to come with us, but she'd said she had things to do at home. Blaire said she closed herself off whenever she wasn't working at the club. It was getting worse instead of better for her, clearly.

"I'll see y'all later," I told them, and stepped out of the car.

The front door opened before my foot had hit the bottom step, and Grant was waiting for me at the top of the stairs. His face was full of concern and fear. In my heart, I knew what I had seen earlier wasn't his fault. It still hadn't made it easier to watch. I hadn't been able to ease his mind when I had left him at the club. I was upset, and I wasn't sorry about that. He would be, too, if he'd been in my position. But from the look on his face, he had worried about this all day.

"I'm sorry," we both said in unison.

Grant frowned. "Why are *you* sorry?" he asked as I stopped in front of him.

"For making you worry all day. I shouldn't have done that. It was wrong of me."

Grant let out a groan and rubbed his face with his hand. "Harlow, please don't make this worse. I already feel like a complete ass, and you apologizing sweetly is making me feel like a bigger one."

I reached up and tugged his hand away from his face. "You shouldn't have let her get so close to you. In the future, be more guarded. But it was a mistake, and I understand that. I don't think you wanted her to kiss you."

He pulled me toward him and pressed me against the door as his mouth covered mine. The mint flavor of his mouth made me wonder how many times he'd brushed his teeth. Smiling against his lips, I slid an arm around his neck and licked at the corner of his mouth, then pulled his tongue into my mouth and sucked on it.

Grant's hands were under my top in seconds. They cupped my breasts as he pressed his erection against my stomach. This was just what I needed after a day of thinking about Nan's lips on Grant.

He broke the kiss, and I had started to argue when he jerked the door open. "Get inside before we get arrested for indecent exposure," he growled.

Laughing, I hurried inside but didn't get far before Grant had me pressed against the wall as he kissed my neck and took little bites of my shoulder. I could feel the hardness he'd teased me with outside against my bottom as he ground his hips in a circular motion. All I could do was put both of my hands against the wall to hold myself upright and enjoy the ride.

He pulled my shorts down my legs, along with my panties, and I obediently stepped out of them. Then his hands were on my bottom, cupping it as he moved my legs apart. Before I could figure out what he was doing, his mouth was on my slit. I cried out and fell against the wall as his tongue danced along the tender folds.

"Oh, God, I can't stand up," I cried out, feeling my knees buckle.

Grant reached up, grabbed my waist, and turned me around. "Put your legs over my shoulders," he said, looking up at me while he held me by the waist. "I got you. I won't let you fall."

I did as he instructed, and he held my hips and pushed me back against the wall before continuing his efforts to drive me crazy. I grabbed at the one thing I seemed so fond of when he did this: his hair. He seemed to like it. His kissing always got more intense when I started tugging on his thick locks.

I panted and let out moans and gasps, not caring if I fell off his shoulders. Just as long as he kept doing this. Just when I was about to shatter, he stopped, and his eyes found mine. "You ready to come?"

I nodded, afraid I would scream yes if I opened my mouth.

Grant grinned wickedly, then stuck his tongue out at me before lowering his head and flicking the tip over my most sensitive spot three times and pulling it into his mouth and sucking. I completely lost it. I was sure the neighbors heard my cries. But I didn't care.

Grant

The next day, at the doctor's office, Harlow lay on the examination table with her shirt pulled up, her bare stomach exposed for the ultrasound. It was still flat. You couldn't tell there was anything inside. She looked normal. Well, as normal as a very anxious person can look. She had spent all morning cooking breakfast, even though she never cooked breakfast. Then she'd spent an hour trying to decide what to wear. I could tell she was nervous, but you would have thought we were going to be introduced to the baby and she wanted to make a good impression.

We were at the doctor's office to hear the heartbeat. I had Googled the process and discovered that if we didn't hear the heartbeat, that meant the baby hadn't made it that far. Harlow hadn't had any bleeding or cramping, but apparently, that didn't mean she couldn't have miscarried.

Miscarrying this baby would devastate her. The idea of seeing her brokenhearted wasn't something I wanted, but I wasn't sure what I wanted to hear today. I just wanted Harlow to be OK. Safe. I needed her to be safe. And happy. I just wasn't sure there was a way for me to have both.

Again, I was completely helpless. I hated this feeling.

"OK, are you ready?" the doctor asked, looking down at Harlow. Somehow he knew not to ask me, because he knew I wasn't ready. If we heard a heartbeat and it was healthy, that meant this wasn't over, that I had to continue living in fear of losing Harlow. But if we didn't hear a heartbeat, the pain she would endure might be too much for her to bear.

"Yes," Harlow said. The excitement and nervousness in her voice weren't lost on the doctor. He smiled reassuringly. He did this all the time. He seemed positive, which was good. Or wasn't. Hell, I didn't know what was good anymore.

Then it happened. The sound that changed it all.

A rapid, steady thumping filled the room, and all I could do was stare down at Harlow's stomach. Her hand reached out and grabbed mine tightly, and she let out a sob that startled me. I looked up at her, and she was smiling so damn big, but her eyes were filled with unshed tears. The wonderment on her face said everything I was thinking. There was a life in there. One we had created. It was real.

"Sounds strong. That's a very good sign," the doctor said.

Harlow's hand squeezed mine, and she laughed. The heartbeat sped up a second with her laughter, then went back to normal. Had the baby heard her laugh?

"I think this is a good start. I feel positive about this. You look good. I've studied your records, and as you know, we had to change up your medications. Some things you can't take while pregnant, but I feel sure this will work out just fine. You call me if you feel funny at any time. Don't wait. Call me." He turned his focus on me. "She needs to call me immediately," he repeated.

"Yes, sir," I replied. Not something he had to demand of me. The second I thought she was having problems, I'd call the ambulance, then I'd call him.

He pulled the monitoring equipment up, and I pulled Harlow's shirt down and helped her sit up, but not before kissing her nose. I had to kiss her somewhere. She held on to my arm for a moment, that huge, brilliant smile still in place. "We heard it," she said, as if to reassure me that we had heard the baby's heartbeat.

"Yeah, we did," I said.

How was I supposed to not want that? How could I choose anyone or anything over Harlow? I was a mess. A confused mess. I loved that sound because it was us. Our baby. It also made her so damn happy. Was I being selfish not to want her to have this because I might lose her?

The doctor told Harlow some more things about her new medications and said that she should continue with moderate exercise as long as she rested often. She assured him that she would, and then we were escorted out through the back entrance again.

When we were in the truck and headed back to Rosemary Beach, Harlow scooted close to me. "That was amazing," she said softly.

I didn't want to agree with her, but she was right. It was. "Yeah, I know."

She wrapped her arms around one of mine and laid her head on my shoulder. "In about two more months, we'll find out if it's a boy or a girl, and we'll be able to see it move."

A boy or a girl . . . see it move . . . I wanted those things. I wanted them with her. Only her. But I couldn't forget the risk. Was this the way it was supposed to be in life? You couldn't have every dream, but you could have part of it? You could only have a taste of something but never the full thing?

My precious baby,

Today we heard your heartbeat. It was the most beautiful sound in the world. I've never felt so much joy. Until that moment, I didn't know that much joy was possible for one human to process. My heart was bursting with love. Knowing that you were in there. That you were safe.

Your daddy said that when I laughed, your heart rate sped up as if you heard me. I hope you did. You make me so very happy. You aren't even here, and my life is so full.

I've never seen your father quite so moved, either. He didn't say much, but the wonder in his eyes as the sound of your beating heart filled the room was something I will never forget. I will carry it with me forever. You became real to him today.

Don't get me wrong. He loved you before. He just didn't know how much until he heard you. He doesn't have the connection we have yet, because you're safely tucked inside of me. You will bond with him soon enough, though. You will be the reason he laughs and finds joy in life. I just hope I get to see it.

But remember, if I don't, I will be there in spirit. I promise to make a deal with heaven to get a front-row seat to your life. I want to see the two people I love most in the world experience this lifetime together. If I'm there with you right now, you know how much I love you, because I'll be crying as you read this, just as I'm crying happy tears right now.

Your life was blessed before you even arrived. No matter how God determines my fate, you won't be alone. You will do great things, and I will be watching you and cheering you on, either right there beside you or above the clouds.

Love you always,
Mommy

Harlow

Blaire sat at the table trying to get Nate to eat his dinner. He wasn't interested. He was focused on the door his daddy and his uncle Grant had just walked through.

"You have to eat," Blaire told him as he slammed his small hands on the high chair in frustration.

"No! Dada!" he shouted.

Blaire rolled her eyes. " 'No' is his new word of the week. If I've heard 'no' once this week, I've heard it a million times. That and 'Dada' seem to be his favorite words. Last week, it was 'cah' and 'Dada,' 'cah' meaning car, which means he wants to go in the car. The kid likes to go."

I smiled and watched as he pointed at the door and demanded, "Dada," again. He was very fond of his father.

"I give up," Blaire said, setting down the bowl of oatmeal she had been trying to get him to eat. "Let me see if Rush minds taking him outside with them."

Nate watched his mother walk to the door with complete concentration until he realized I was still seated on the other side of him. He swung his silver eyes my way and gave me a toothless grin. The older he got, the more he looked like his dad. Which I was sure was a good thing for all the female babies of the world. One day, there would be another Finlay man available.

Blaire came back inside, followed by Rush. His eyes went straight to Nate. "You want me, little man?" he said, grinning as if he didn't already know the answer.

"Take the oatmeal with you, and see if you can get him to eat it while y'all do your male bonding," Blaire said.

Rush unbuckled Nate, who was now clapping happily, and took the bowl Blaire was holding out for him. He bent down and kissed Blaire. I turned my head when I saw the tip of his tongue swipe her bottom lip.

"I got this guy. He'll eat for me. You two talk. Grant and I will teach Nate about the world."

Blaire laughed as she sat back down. "Oh, good Lord. That doesn't sound good."

Rush winked and sauntered back out of the house with the baby and a bowl of oatmeal in his arms. He didn't look anything like a daddy, with his tattoo-covered arms, but he was a really good one. He was how I pictured Grant being.

"I'd ask you if you wanted some coffee, but that's off-limits," Blaire said, leaning back in her chair with a sigh. "How are things? Is Grant doing OK with everything?"

I wasn't sure how to answer this. It had been two weeks since we had heard the heartbeat, and he was much better. He even called it a baby now. Before, he had acted as if it didn't exist. The baby was real to him now. I had seen it in his eyes the moment it clicked for him. But he was still edgy. And he was determined to make sure I was well taken care of. "Hearing the heartbeat helped him. I think he gets it now, at least somewhat. He understands what I'm feeling, that there's a life in there that we made, and I can't just end it. I don't think he would fight me if I decided to end the pregnancy tomorrow, but he does have some connection to the baby now. That's a start."

Blaire frowned. She wasn't a frowner, so seeing her frown was strange. "He's scared of losing you. I think right now, he'd sacrifice anyone other than you. He loves you." Her face transformed from the frown to a smile. "And I am so happy he found you. I always knew Grant was so much more than the women he paraded in and out of his bedroom."

I tried not to flinch.

Blaire squeezed her eyes tightly closed. "I'm so sorry! I shouldn't have said that. I just . . . I know what Rush's past was like firsthand. I actually saw him having sex with one of his many one-night stands before we were dating. And I saw him heavily making out with another one. And I saw another one leaving his room one morning. I guess I'm immune to Rush's past. It was before me, and it doesn't bother me. But you didn't see all of that with Grant. I need to watch my tongue."

I hadn't known Blaire had seen Rush having sex with another woman. Even if it was before her, that still seemed awful. But then, their relationship didn't start out in a typical way. They were stepsiblings, and Blaire had been dumped into Rush's lap by her dad without Rush's consent.

"It's fine. I know what Grant was like. I did hear him having sex with Nan; I just can't imagine seeing it."

Blaire shuddered. "I don't want the visual, either, so let's change the subject. Are you going to find out the sex of the baby?"

We were. I wanted to know, just in case I didn't get that

chance to hold my baby. I wanted to know what I was having. I wanted to name it and talk to it. I also wanted to stop calling it an *it*. "Yes. We're going to find out."

Blaire smiled. "I loved knowing what Nate was before he arrived. I was able to daydream about him and talk to him, and of course, Rush decorated his room for him. Wait . . . where will you put the baby?"

There was no extra room in Grant's condo. I had thought about moving the dresser in the bedroom out into the living room and putting the baby's crib there. But we didn't even have a crib yet. I had no idea what our plans were. "I'm not sure yet. We'll have to make room in the bedroom for the crib."

As much as I didn't want to think about the worst case, I had to plan for it. I couldn't leave Grant without any preparation. I knew Maryann was ready to step up and take the baby if she had to. I was secure knowing that if Grant couldn't handle it or didn't want that sole responsibility, Maryann was prepared. But I wanted Grant to keep our baby. I wanted our baby to chant "Dada" over and over again and raise its little arms at the sight of Grant. I just couldn't be sure that was what would happen, especially not right away.

If he needed to grieve.

"Your thoughts just went downhill. It's all over your face. What did I say?" Blaire was so observant. I needed to be careful. I didn't want her thinking I was preparing to die. I didn't want anyone to think that, because I intended to live. I just wasn't living in a fairy tale, and I knew that it was possible I wasn't strong enough.

"I'm sorry. Sometimes I overplan in my head. I like to be prepared for everything," I explained, and forced a smile I didn't feel.

Grant

Rush came back outside, with Nate in his arms and a bowl of something. Nate spotted me and clapped. "Yeah, that's your gullible uncle Grant who keeps picking up the shit you drop."

"He's gonna end up cursing around Blaire, and you're gonna be sleeping on the couch for a week. Maybe she'll stick your ass under the stairs. I hear payback is a bitch," I told him, referring to how Blaire had slept in a room under Rush's stairs when she first came to town.

He rolled his eyes, sat down, and put Nate on his knee. "If he says one of those words, we'll blame it on Uncle Grant, won't we, buddy? Point your finger that way, and save Daddy's ass," Rush said with a smirk.

"What's in the bowl?" I asked as he held a spoonful up to Nate's mouth. He turned his head away. Smart kid. It looked nasty.

"Oatmeal. He hates it," Rush said, trying to get Nate to take a mouthful.

"If he hates it, and I would hate it, too, why are you feeding it to him?" I asked.

Rush lifted his eyes to me. "Because Blaire said to. You don't question the mommy. Ever."

Good to know.

"So you heard the heartbeat," Rush said, putting the oat-meal down in a sign of defeat.

"Yeah. We did. And . . . well, it felt real finally. Like there was something there. A life. It wasn't just Harlow—there was another heartbeat inside of her. A heartbeat we created. I just . . . is it wrong that I felt attached to it? That I wanted to protect it? I can't lose Harlow. I can't. So I shouldn't feel this way, right?"

Rush looked down at Nate and pressed a kiss to the top of his head. "You're asking a man who has a kid. A man who would throw himself in front of a bullet, a truck, you fucking name it—I would do whatever I had to for this boy. He's mine. I can't ever consider not wanting him. But again, Blaire's life was never threatened. We didn't have that kind of decision to make. But no, I don't think it's wrong that you felt something when you heard the heartbeat. I cried like a damn baby when I saw the first ultrasound of Nate. It's an emotional thing. It's normal. Don't beat yourself up for loving something you created with the woman you love. Especially if she adores it."

I heard him, and he made sense, but I was still tormented by the idea that this life I was growing attached to could take Harlow's life away. She was my number one. "If I lose her, it's my fault. I did this. I wasn't careful, and now she's pregnant," I said. He had heard me say this before, but it was haunting me, and I needed to say it. I couldn't say it to her. And hav-ing Kiro tell me this exact same thing only confirmed it. I did this.

"You didn't know she had health problems. She was scared to tell you, and I understand that, but I also know that you can't blame yourself for something you didn't know."

I had always been careful. Never sleeping with anyone without protection. I'd never considered going without a wrapper, but Harlow had gotten under my skin, and I was so damn crazy about her that I lost all rational thought. My lust for her made me make bad decisions. But did my not knowing about her heart actually change anything? No. It was still the same outcome. I did this.

🎴

Last night, Harlow had lain in my arms, and I'd watched her eyes study the room. Finally, she had said we would need to move the dresser into the living room to fit the baby's crib. I hadn't responded. I hadn't known how. I liked the idea of bringing the baby home and Harlow rocking it, holding it, and putting it to bed. But I was afraid to live in that world. Because if that wasn't the outcome, I needed to be prepared to take on Harlow's role, too.

She kissed me good-bye this morning when I left for work, then she rolled over and went back to sleep. Seeing her get some rest eased my worries a little.

But I hadn't told her the truth about where I was going.

I wasn't working; I was house hunting. If Harlow could live by sheer force of will, I decided I was going to give her the world to fight for. Starting with a house and a bedroom she could decorate for our baby. We could paint it together and pick out the furniture, although I was going to go along with anything she said. Unless, of course, it was a boy and she tried to put girlie shit in his room.

I parked my truck outside of the house I wanted to buy for her—for us. It wasn't as big as what she was used to, but Harlow wasn't one to expect luxury. She had grown up with her grandmother in a modest home in North Carolina.

The light blue house was farther out from the water than I wanted—beachfront properties were out of my price range—but it was in a quaint little gated community. The houses weren't too close together, but it was still a neighborhood of sorts. A coastal one. I had driven by this house on more than one occasion and admired it. The white fence around it and the wraparound porch with large hurricane shutters made it look like an old Florida plantation, but it was smaller and only a few years old. The owner had built it and never moved in. It had been on the market since then. I had always thought it was a shame that no one ever used the swing in the large oak tree in the front yard or enjoyed the rocking chairs on the front porch. It was just empty.

Rush's Range Rover pulled up beside me, and I opened my truck door. I had called him after I'd gone to the real estate office that was selling the house and gotten a key. The office handled a lot of the sales for the condos I built, so they didn't mind handing over the key.

Rush stepped out, looked up at the house and back at me, and grinned. "I feel like I'm in Mayberry. It even has a fucking tree swing."

Laughing, I walked through the gate and stepped into the front yard. "Question is, do you think she'll like it?" I asked him as I took the four steps leading up to the porch two at a time.

"I think she'll love it," Rush said, following me.

I unlocked the door, and we stepped inside. The entryway was small but had high ceilings with exposed beams. A staircase was to the left, and a hallway leading into the living room was straight ahead. We walked into the living room, which had a large fireplace with a big sturdy mantel as its focal point. The hardwood floors were tongue-and-groove, which only made the older coastal feel of the house more authentic. There was an arched doorway leading into the kitchen and dining room to the right and then another arched doorway to what looked like a sunroom to the left.

"How many bedrooms?" Rush asked as he looked out to the backyard. It was fenced in and had plenty of space for a swing set and maybe a pool when the baby was older.

"Agent said it was a four-bedroom. All upstairs."

"Might want to check those out. They could make or break the place."

I nodded, and we headed upstairs. The board-and-batten walls were a nice touch; I knew they cost a little more than basic Sheetrock. The room directly to the right was a guest bedroom. It wasn't that big, but it had a walk-in closet and a small private bathroom. We walked to the next room, which was larger, with an even bigger walk-in closet. It was joined by a connecting bathroom to another room identical to it. Then to the far right was the master bedroom. It had its own fireplace and a Jacuzzi tub in the bathroom. The place was nicer than I expected. I hoped they'd take my offer and come down on the asking price a little.

"I think it's perfect," Rush said as we walked through the attic space.

"Me, too."

"Guess it's time you called and made an offer."

I couldn't wait to show Harlow. To enjoy watching her decorate the place. We could make a lifetime of memories here. I wanted a lifetime of memories with her. This was the perfect setting.

My precious baby,

I spent the day looking at cribs. I had no idea there were so many of them. Finding the one that will be perfect for you is going to be harder than I thought. So I walked away without buying one. But I didn't walk away empty-handed.

Since we don't know if you're a boy or a girl yet, I decided that I had better buy an outfit for each scenario. If you're a girl, then you wore the soft pink gown with the white trim and matching bonnet home from the hospital. And if you're a boy, you wore the sea-blue romper with the baseball and bat on the front. I bought both of those outfits today, just in case.

I probably could have waited until I knew what you would be, but I was too excited. Seeing all those little outfits and feeling the soft fabric had me imagining you and daydreaming about the day I would get to hold you.

I expect I will get to do a lot of that, since you'll be sleeping in our room. I'm already planning on where I'll put your crib. I think you'll like a view of the water. Maybe we can make that work.

It really doesn't matter where you sleep, because no matter where it is, you will always be safe, cherished, and loved.

Love you always,
Mommy

Harlow

Grant was anxious. I had never seen him like this. He kept watching me nervously and smiling like he had something big he wanted to tell me. It was completely odd behavior for him.

It was distracting me that I wasn't the one acting like a nervous ninny this time. When we had listened to the baby's heartbeat the first time, I barely had been able to contain myself that day before the appointment. But this day, the day we finally got to see our baby and find out if it was a boy or a girl, it was Grant who couldn't sit still.

I had gone through an ultrasound before, but it wasn't one like this one. The first one had been very basic, so they could see the baby and hear the heartbeat internally. This time, it would be a 3-D machine that would allow us to actually see the baby's facial features. The nurse walked into the small room where we were waiting, followed by the doctor.

"You two ready?" he asked with a bright smile on his face.

"Yes," I replied, but Grant didn't say anything. He seemed tense. I reached up and rubbed his arm to try to ease his strained expression. This wasn't going to hurt me or the baby.

"Good, let's see if we can find out what we're having here," the doctor said as he sat down on a stool. "Normally, the nurse does this, but I want to check some things while you're here. I brought her along in case I forget something," he explained.

I turned my attention back to Grant, whose complete focus was on the currently blank screen.

"You OK?" I asked. He dropped his gaze to mine.

"Yeah, I'm good. Are you?" he asked, suddenly realizing he hadn't checked on me in the past few minutes while we were waiting. He was more than overprotective. Since my belly had started to show, he had gotten a little crazy with the hovering thing.

The doctor moved the device over my stomach and nodded his head toward the screen. "Here we go," he said as an image of our baby began to appear.

Grant's hand gripped mine tighter as the screen very clearly showed two little feet stuck up in the air.

I couldn't form words as the doctor chuckled. "Well, that was easy to spot. She's making it very easy."

She.

That one word was more powerful than I could have imagined.

She.

I sniffled and blinked rapidly, trying hard to clear my vision so I could see her.

"Look there, she's found her fingers, and she likes them. You may have a thumb sucker," the doctor said as he showed us our little girl sucking three fingers into her mouth.

I was unable to keep the part-laughter, part-sob from escaping.

"And it looks like she has all her fingers and toes. Her heartbeat still sounds really strong," the doctor assured us. I hadn't even noticed the sound—I was so taken in by just watching her—but it was there in its perfect, pumping little rhythm.

"Did you feel that?" the doctor asked me.

I didn't want to look away from the screen. "What?" I asked.

"A strong fluttering feeling . . . *there*. Did you feel it?"

I had felt it. I had been feeling it for the past couple of weeks. I had thought it was bad gas.

"Yes," I said, watching as she kicked seconds after I felt the fluttering feeling.

"The 3-D isn't real time. It's delayed. So you're seeing her kick a few seconds after she does it," the doctor explained.

"When can I feel it?" Grant asked, speaking up for the first time. I tore my eyes from our daughter to see him watching the screen in complete fascination.

"Give it a couple weeks, and you'll feel it," the doctor assured Grant.

For the next fifteen minutes, we sat there watching our little girl wiggle and go from sucking her fingers to her thumb. She also liked to stick her foot up to touch her head. She was perfect.

And I had thought I couldn't love her more. How very wrong I was.

⌘

Grant passed the turn-off for home, and I glanced over at him. We had sat in awed silence for most of the drive. Every once in a while, one of us would ask if the other had seen her do something, and then we would fall silent again. I couldn't wait to write to her about this moment, because this time, I knew she was a she.

"I have something I want to show you," he said when he caught me staring at him.

"Um, OK," I replied, not sure what it could be that required him to drive to the outer town limits of Rosemary Beach. Maybe we were going to the club. I really hoped not. I just wanted to go home and think about our little girl.

Grant didn't turn toward the club but instead pulled into a gated community that I had always noticed from afar but had never been inside. The houses were all beautiful coastal places that I assumed were mostly owned by out-of-towners who came for vacation or rented them out.

Grant touched a card to the black box, and the gate slowly opened. I wondered if he was building something here, although it didn't look like any new developments were happening, nor did Grant normally deal in single-residence houses.

We rounded a circle on the road paved with split brick, which I thought was really cool. Then he pulled into a driveway in front of a blue house that looked like it belonged on the front cover of *Coastal Living* magazine.

Were we visiting someone?

"What do you think?" he asked. The nervousness from earlier in the day was back in his voice.

What did I think? "About the house?" I asked.

He nodded.

I didn't have to look at it again to know I thought it was an ideal house for a family . . . but wait. Surely not. I fought back excitement at the idea that Grant was considering buying this house for us, and I reminded myself that we were perfectly happy in his condo. We didn't need a house, even if it was as absolutely perfect as this one.

"I think it's a beautiful place," I said carefully. I didn't want him to think I'd gotten my hopes up. It would upset him if he thought I wasn't happy where we were, and I didn't want him to be any more stressed.

"You do?" he asked, still studying my every expression.

I nodded.

He opened his truck door and got out. "Let's go inside," he said, before closing his door and walking around to help me as I stepped down on my side.

We were going inside? Did that mean he wanted me to see the inside, or were there people in there? I wanted to get excited, but I was afraid to. I wasn't sure why we were here.

Grant produced a key and opened the door. It swung wide, and he motioned for me to step inside. I walked in slowly. The first thing I noticed was that it was completely empty. The second thing I noticed was that it was breathtaking. The vaulted ceilings and attention to detail were fantastic.

"Come with me," he said, taking my hand as we headed directly for the stairs. Upstairs, we walked through a large open space that could be a sitting area or even a game room. Then Grant opened one of the doors, and we walked into a large bedroom with pale pink walls and a chandelier. From the windows, you could see the Gulf across the street and the backyard, which was not only a nice big space but also fenced in.

I turned around to see Grant running a hand through his hair nervously and watching me.

"It's a great room. But I don't understand," I said, needing some clarification, even though my excitement was quickly growing.

He glanced down at my stomach, then back up at me. "Would you want this to be her room?"

Her room.

Meaning we would live here.

The waterworks were threatening to take over, and I blinked back tears and sucked in a breath to keep from sobbing on him.

"Is it for sale?" I asked, realizing that I hadn't seen a for-sale sign in the yard.

"No," he replied, and my heart sank. "Not anymore." He held up the keys he'd used to get in. "It's already ours."

It took me all of two seconds to fling myself into his arms before I burst into tears.

Grant

We didn't go back to the apartment that night. I called Rush to help me move the bed over, and we stayed the night in our new house. Harlow was too giddy to leave, and I was too damn happy watching her. I had been afraid she would be overwhelmed or maybe not like it.

But I had worried for nothing.

I felt like the king of the fucking world.

The next week, I had movers come to the condo and help us pack up, because I didn't want Harlow bending and lifting anything. We slowly moved our things in and got settled into our new home. And that was what it was. I had a home now. A real one. For the first time in my life, I had a real home. A real family. My family.

The weekly doctor visits kept me hopeful, and the fear slowly started to fade. Harlow believed, without a doubt, that she would make it through this, and she was already thinking about the swing set we would pick out for Lila Kate.

We had spent an entire week sitting up searching for baby names on the Internet before we agreed on one. Even if I hadn't liked the name Lila Kate at the time, I would have learned to love it after hearing Harlow say it when she spoke to her now-round stomach. It still wasn't very big, but you could definitely tell she was pregnant.

I had expected her to worry over looking fat or to be self-conscious, but she never did, and she never was. She would stand in front of the mirror and look at herself, then smile up at me like this was the best thing in the world. She was going to be a wonderful mother.

Then, one day, while I was putting together the baby's crib in the master bedroom, I heard Harlow shout from the bathroom, "Grant! Hurry!" A million horrible thoughts ran through my mind, so I was expecting the worst when I found a smiling Harlow soaking in a bubble bath. I took a deep breath and told myself to calm the fuck down. I couldn't believe something bad was about to happen every time she called for me.

"She's moving," Harlow whispered, as if talking might cause her to stop. "Come feel."

I had been waiting for this. Harlow had felt her daily, but so far, I hadn't been there at the right time. I knelt down beside the tub, and she took my hand and placed it on her stomach.

"Here, press down just a bit so she'll push back," she said softly.

I did as I was told, and sure enough, a gentle little kick was my response. The grin that broke across my face was so damn big it hurt my cheeks. I had a little fighter in there. She was strong like her momma.

"Isn't that amazing?" Harlow asked as I held my hand against her stomach and felt Lila Kate moving around. I had obviously annoyed her, so now she was pretty active.

"She's spunky," I said, and Harlow threw back her head and

laughed. Lila Kate kicked again and pushed against me. It was like she wanted to join us. Maybe she heard Harlow laughing and wanted out so she could be a part of this moment.

"Talk to her," Harlow said.

I had seen Harlow talking to her stomach a lot lately. But I wasn't sure I could do that. I had seen the ultrasound, and I could feel her. She was real to me, but talking to her seemed difficult. I was putting myself out there to love yet another person I could lose.

"I don't know what to say," I told her, hoping that she would drop it.

"Just tell her hello and that you love her. It doesn't have to be profound. She recognizes your voice now. I'm sure of it. She'll know you're talking to her."

Harlow had a lot of faith in this tiny little baby inside her. I agreed that she reacted to Harlow's laughter, but I wasn't sure she actually recognized my voice. It was probably no more than a muffled sound to her right now.

"Please, say something," Harlow pleaded, and I knew I wasn't going to get out of this. She wanted me to talk to our daughter, and I couldn't tell her no.

I cleared my throat and bent closer to Harlow's stomach. "How you doing in there?" I asked, then glanced up to see a very amused Harlow. "I imagine you're ready to get out and stretch. Gotta be cramped in that little space you got." Harlow was still watching me expectantly.

She wanted me to tell our baby I loved her. Saying that aloud would make it real. It would make the fact that I was once again vulnerable to another person real. How could I keep her safe, too? What if I had to do it alone? Closing my eyes, I pushed that thought away. I wouldn't think about it. I refused to.

"I love you, Lila Kate. I can't wait to hold you and watch you sleep in your mother's arms. If you're lucky, you'll look just like her." There, I'd said it. Exactly what I was thinking. Exactly how I felt. I had laid myself bare.

"I hope she looks like you," Harlow said, cupping my face in her hands. "You're the pretty one."

I lowered my mouth to hers and whispered just before I captured her sweet lips, "No one will ever be more beautiful than you."

Harlow lifted her sudsy, wet arm and wrapped it around my neck and deepened the kiss while I soaked in the silky warmth of her touch. She could make everything better with a kiss. Fear and worry vanished when she was close to me.

"Get in with me," she said, and started tugging on my shirt. I didn't argue. I removed my shirt, then got rid of my jeans and boxers, before climbing in behind her. She turned around to straddle me, her ever-larger breasts covered in bubbles. This was quite possibly the best bath product ever invented. At least, for the male species. I filled my hands with her tits just as she sank down onto my hard length. When she had me completely buried inside her, she arched her back, causing those fantastic play toys to jiggle and sway.

"You're in control, sweet girl. Take it how you want it," I told her while enjoying the beautiful view.

She leaned back and put her hands on my legs. I couldn't have asked for a better position. Then she took it a step further and began to bounce slowly up and down on me. I wanted my hands full of her boobs, but then they'd stop that hypnotic movement, so I grabbed her waist instead and helped her ride me.

"I could watch these titties all damn day," I said as she moaned and slammed down on me harder.

Unable to withstand it any longer, I reached out and squeezed them, feeling the pebbled hardness of her nipples against my palms. She cried out my name, and it made me even crazier.

"Ride it, sweet girl. Show me what makes you feel good. That hot little pussy is my fucking nirvana. You know you've got me so wrapped up in you I can't see anything or anyone else. Just you. Just you."

"Oh, God, I'm gonna come. Keep talking naughty," she panted as she reached up and covered my hands with hers.

"Soaking-wet pussy is swollen and horny all the damn time. I want to slip my fingers in those tiny panties and play with it every time I look at you. Taste you and smell you. You smell so incredibly sweet." My dirty talk sent her over the edge.

She grabbed my shoulders and began calling out to God and me all at the same time. "That's it, come on my cock," I encouraged her as she trembled and shuddered. "My sweet pussy."

"Oh, God! Stop! I can't take it. I'm so close again," she moaned, leaning into me. Then she clamped down on me, and I lost my restraint.

Grabbing her hair, I yelled out her name and followed her into ecstasy.

My sweet Lila Kate,

Your nursery is almost ready. It's fit for a princess, but then, you are a princess. You're our princess. There has never been another baby girl who is as loved as you are. I'm secretly hoping you look just like your daddy. But no matter who you look like, you will be beautiful.

We can't wait to show you the things we've bought for you. We bought you your first Christmas ornament today. It's white with pink polka dots and your initials monogrammed on the front. When I saw it in all of its sweet little girlie cuteness, I wanted to make sure you had it to hang on the tree every year. That way, if I'm watching from the clouds, you can remember that I picked it out for you. Daddy had the idea to get your initials painted on it. But then, he's a smart man.

I hope that we hang it on the tree together each year. I'll bake cookies, and you can decorate them with icing and sprinkles. Then we'll string the popcorn and make a mess with glitter and glue as we decorate our own ornaments. It will be the most loved tree in Rosemary Beach. We'll invite Nate over to help us. I'm sure he'll enjoy making a mess as much as you will.

I've been stocking your library with all of my favorite picture books. I've written a note in each one from me to you, and I've added the dates that I bought the books, in case I'm not there to share them with you. Your daddy will read them to you. He can tell you about all the places I took him to in search of the perfect books for you.

The weeks are ticking by, and before I know it, I'll see your face. If we have a lifetime or only a few moments together, you will be the most important thing that ever happens to me in this life.

Love you always,
Mommy

Harlow

We were attending a fund-raiser ball at the club tonight to raise money for the local fire department. Rosemary Beach wasn't a big town, and the nearest big city was a forty-five-minute drive away, so the volunteer fire department was very cherished and necessary.

Woods had decided to host the ball, though the truth was, many residents had plenty of money to give to the fire department outright—and many did. That's how it had gotten its start. But they liked to attend big galas so they could dress up and spend the evening with important people like Rush's dad. Dean Finlay, the drummer for Slacker Demon and my father's best friend, was on the board of directors for the Kerrington Country Club. He wasn't your typical board member, but then, neither were Grant and Rush, and they were also board members. When Woods had inherited the club from his father after he died, he fired all of the other board members and chose his own. He and his father had never seen eye-to-eye on anything.

Senator Barnes would also be in attendance. I wasn't sure of everyone who had made the invitation list, but I had heard his name from Woods recently. I hadn't been spending much time at the club now that Nan was back in town. I was enjoying our house and preparing for Lila Kate. Dealing with the social dynamics of the Kerrington Club was something I wanted to keep my distance from right now. I spent time with Blaire at her house or mine; same with Della.

But tonight Grant had to fulfill his duties as a board member and needed to be there. Finding a dress that fit me was another story. My stomach was really showing now. I was thirty-one weeks along, and both Lila Kate and I were doing well. She was moving more and more lately; she'd started pushing her little foot so hard I could see my stomach stick out in that spot. Grant was highly entertained when this happened. Made it worth the discomfort to hear his laughter while he watched her beat me up. Honestly, I wouldn't trade one of those moments. Ever.

With Blaire's help, I had found a knee-length black crepe empire-waist gown with a crystal-encrusted halter neckline. I wore it with a pair of silver Louboutins. How was it that I had never felt beautiful before, but now that my stomach was the size of a basketball, I suddenly felt better about myself?

"Wow." Grant's voice interrupted my thoughts, and I glanced up in the mirror to see him walking up behind me. His eyes gleamed with appreciation. I let my eyes travel down his body, wrapped perfectly in a tuxedo. I had seen him in one before, and I knew how devastatingly handsome he could be, but this time, he was mine. And when the night was over, I would get to undress him. All mine.

"If I wasn't a board member," he said, before his lips touched my bare shoulder, "I would keep you here, and you could wear that sexy little dress, and we could play striptease. You strip, and I watch." His wicked grin made me laugh.

"Sounds like I would be doing all the work," I retorted.

He wiggled his eyebrows suggestively. "Trust me, baby, once you got naked, I'd make it totally worth it."

I shrugged. "OK, fine. You talked me into it. Let's stay here and play."

Grant pulled me back against his chest and gazed at me in the mirror. We stood there together, the three of us. My obvious stomach—and Lila Kate's presence—couldn't be missed. I wanted a picture of us, and I wanted it now. Just like this. I could put it with the next letter I wrote to her.

"Where's your phone?" I asked him, looking around for mine.

He reached into his pocket and pulled it out. "Here," he replied.

"I want a picture of us. The three of us. Like we are right now," I told him.

"OK," he said, pulling me close to him, my back to his chest. "I think I can hold it up and point it down so it'll catch your adorable bump."

"It's not a bump. It's a beach ball. Just be honest," I said.

He winked. "You never tell a woman that her stomach looks like a beach ball. The results can be dangerous. Now, look up at the phone. This may take a few tries." He tried three times before he was able to get us both smiling and my stomach in clear view. I loved it.

"Text it to me. I want it, too," I told him.

He nodded and quickly sent me the photo. I would look at it later when I found my phone.

"You know we can get someone to take better pictures of us tonight if you want," he said.

I loved our selfie with Lila Kate, but that wasn't a bad idea. I would ask Blaire to take some pictures of us tonight. Then I'd have several to put with the letters.

⊞

The Fireman's Ball was a success. There were hundreds of people there, and each had paid a lot for a ticket. I foresaw new fire trucks in the near future for Rosemary Beach.

Grant kept me close to his side while he greeted people and made introductions. There were so many people I hadn't met yet. Watching Grant like this made me even more proud of him. He could go from sexy playboy to businessman in the blink of an eye—although the only playing he was doing these days was with me.

"I'm going to find Dean. Rush is looking for him. There're some influential people here tonight who Woods wants to become members of the club, and he thinks Dean might seal the deal. Will you be OK by yourself for a few minutes? I don't see Blaire anywhere, but I see Della over there near the corner talking to Bethy and Jimmy."

I preferred to visit with Della, Bethy, and Jimmy instead of people I didn't know. Several strangers seemed to recognize me, and they all zeroed in on my stomach with wide eyes. I was sure this would somehow make it into the gossip magazines. I expected someone to Tweet a photo of me and share with the world that I was knocked up. I had managed to keep a low profile, but with this crowd, I wasn't sure if that was possible.

"So you're still pregnant. Like, you're actually gonna go through with this." Nan's voice brought me to a stop, and I wasn't sure if I should acknowledge her or keep walking. I wanted to keep the peace with her. I had no reason to be mad at her, and I knew she would forever hate me, but retaliating would only make me stoop to her level. So I faced her.

"Yes, I'm going through with it," I answered simply. She didn't deserve any explanation.

She frowned, then let out an exasperated sigh. "What, dear old Dad didn't force you to get an abortion so he could save his favorite child?" The bitterness in her voice made me sad. She was mean, but she hadn't exactly been given the best life. Our father had shown me love as a child; he hadn't done the same for Nan.

"Kiro can't make me do anything. This is my baby. Not his. And this baby's life is more important to me than my own," I told her.

She studied me for a moment, as if trying to decide what I meant by that. "You really mean that, don't you?" she asked.

I nodded. "Yes, I do."

For a brief moment, I thought maybe, just maybe, we were having a breakthrough. Maybe we could bond, or at least call a truce. It was too much to hope that we could actually be family. But then she shrugged and rolled her eyes. "Whatever. It's your life," she said, then sauntered away in her heels. I was almost positive she was wearing a Valentino dress. The perfect ice queen.

When I turned back around, Della, Bethy, and Jimmy were gone. I spun around, looking through the crowd for a familiar face, but I didn't see anyone. Fresh air sounded good, so I decided I would step outside and take a breather while Grant searched for Dean.

The cool night air touched my face, and I closed my eyes and enjoyed the moment. So many eyes following my every move had become overwhelming. I wanted to be at home. My favorite thing to do was plant flowers in my backyard with no company except Grant. I really was a recluse.

"Guess the gossip mags were right. She's knocked up. She looks like she's about to pop." A female voice drifted through the darkness. I stepped back into the shadow of the oak tree I was standing beside. I didn't want whoever was talking about me to see me.

"Very pregnant. And it's Grant's. He's stayed by her side all night. Bailey threw herself at him earlier after following him out of the room, and he pushed her away."

The other girl made an annoyed sound. "Whatever. This is just a case of baby mama guilt. It ain't like he's planning on forever with her. Did you see a ring on her finger? No, you didn't."

My stomach tightened up, and I backed farther into the darkness. I wanted to walk away from their cruel words, because they didn't know anything. They didn't know about my heart. They didn't know Grant was protecting himself.

"He sure was ready to propose to Nan last year. She said he had the ring and everything. It's why she cheated on him. She wasn't ready for commitment. I think she regrets that now, but maybe it's not too late. He got that Manning girl pregnant, but that's all he did."

He was going to propose to Nan? He never told me that. He acted as if his time with her hadn't meant anything. That he had been helping her. Had she really broken his heart? Was that why he had never mentioned marriage? I thought it was because of my heart. I just figured we would talk about it after I survived through the pregnancy.

"I saw Nan and him talking earlier. They were awfully close. Besides, doesn't the Manning girl have, like, a heart problem? Can you have kids with a heart problem?"

I had heard enough. I wanted to go home now. Going back into a room full of people, knowing they were thinking similar things, was too much. I just wanted to hide away in our house. Or was it his house? I hadn't bought it. He had. Was I just there until this thing we had was over?

Oh, God. I felt sick to my stomach. I needed to leave. Walking the long way around so the girls who had been talking about me couldn't see me, I made my way over to the valet. I couldn't take Grant's truck. Even though it was a short two-mile ride to the house, I wasn't comfortable with driving right now.

"Hello, Miss Manning, do you need a car brought around?" Henry asked. He was one of the regular valets.

I would not cry in front of poor Henry. "Could you bring a driver around? I need one of the club limos to take me home."

He nodded and motioned with his hand to someone else. I had left my wrap at the coat check, but I had my clutch under my arm, so at least I had a key to the house. Facing Grant right now was not a good idea. But then he would worry about me. I pulled out my phone and sent him a quick text.

Not feeling well. I think I'm done for the evening. Stay and enjoy yourself. Having a club driver take me home.

Just as I hit Send, a black Mercedes sedan pulled up, and Henry opened the door for me. "Have a good evening, Miss Manning," he said.

"Thank you," I replied, and sank down onto the leather seat.

"I was told you wanted to go home, Miss Manning. Is that correct?" the driver asked.

I nodded. "Yes, please," I managed to say, then stared quietly out the window as the car drove me home.

Grant

Not feeling well. I think I'm done for the evening. Stay and
enjoy yourself. Having a club driver take me home.

What the fuck?

I turned and walked back out of the ballroom, ignoring
whoever was calling my name behind me, and started walking to the exit. I dialed Harlow's number. It rang three times,
then went to voice mail. I cringed. I hated voice mail. I hated
getting her voice-mail message. It made me remember a time I
didn't want to remember.

"Would you like your truck, Mr. Carter?" the valet asked as
I dialed her number again.

"When did Har—Miss Manning leave?" I asked him. "And
get my truck. Fast."

"Yes, sir, and Miss Manning just left five minutes ago. Vern
Bower drove her home in one of the club cars, sir."

"Is Vern back yet?" I asked when I got Harlow's voice mail
again.

"Not yet, sir, but he just left—"

"Five minutes ago, yeah, I heard you," I snapped. I wasn't normally rude to the staff, but I was worried. She wouldn't have just left unless she was upset. Something happened. I had left her in that crowd, and someone had said something to upset her.

"Miss Dreyden and Miss Quinton were out here a short while ago talking about things, sir," the young valet said out of the blue. Those were two of Nan's friends. I recognized their last names.

"And?" I asked as he straightened his tie and stood up straighter. He glanced around to make sure we were alone.

"They were discussing Miss Manning's pregnancy, sir, and her relationship—or lack thereof—with you."

Lack thereof? What did he mean by lack thereof? There was no fucking *lack* in our relationship. It was fucking full-blown and all-consuming. "Not sure what you mean," I told him just as my truck pulled up. I would find out from Harlow what those two nosy bitches had said to send her running. I headed for my truck.

"They may have mentioned the lack of a diamond, sir," the valet called out.

I paused and glanced back at him. His face was red, as if he hated telling me something like that. But I understood exactly what he was saying. Harlow never would have admitted to me that she had heard something like that.

"Thank you," I told him.

He nodded. "Yes, sir. Miss Manning is always real nice to me. I didn't like hearing it any more than she did."

That kid was getting a raise. I was calling Woods tomorrow. I glanced at his name tag. "Thanks, Henry. I'll remember that."

Then I jumped into the truck and hurried home.

✖

The front-porch light was on, and so was the bedroom light upstairs. She had gotten home safely. I could at least catch my breath now. I went inside as quickly as possible, then headed straight for the stairs. I could hear the water running, and I knew she was back in her large Jacuzzi tub. The smell of her lavender bath salts hit me as I stepped into our bedroom. Her phone lay forgotten by her clutch on the bed. She hadn't been ignoring me; she'd just been too busy getting her bath ready. At least, I hoped so.

"Harlow," I called out. I didn't want to frighten her by walking into the bathroom unannounced.

She was lying back in the tub, watching me closely. I couldn't tell if she was mad at me or hurt. There was no real expression on her face for me to read. It was like she was closing me off to her feelings. After what we had gone through, and after I had persuaded her to let me back inside her heart, I couldn't go back to being on the outside. I needed to be able to know what she was thinking.

"You left without me," I said as I took the next few steps in her direction. Her toes peeped up and touched the stream of running water from the faucet.

"I wanted you to enjoy yourself," she said softly.

"Not possible if you're not with me," I said, then sat down on the edge of the tub so I was closer to her eye level.

"You'll get your tux wet," she said with a concerned frown.

"Not worried about the tux. I'm worried about you."

She lifted her gaze to meet my eyes. "I'm fine. I was just tired, and all those people just became too much."

Just like I had known. She would never tell me what she had heard. She was either embarrassed or worried that I would think she was pushing me into marriage, into something I didn't want. I wasn't sure which, but I knew her well enough to know that it was one or the other.

Forcing her to tell me wouldn't help her. I just had to prove to her that what those catty girls had said wasn't true. I had already been thinking about a ring and how to ask her. I was scared to push her too far too fast. She didn't need any extra stress. But it wasn't like I wasn't thinking about it. I hadn't bought this house for her to be a live-in girlfriend—I had bought it for us. Harlow, Lila Kate, and me. This was our home.

I thought she understood all that. But then, I also knew how vicious those girls could be, and if they were at all convinced of what they were saying, then it would sound pretty damn convincing to Harlow. I'd thought that shoving Bailey off me and telling Nan that my relationship with Harlow wasn't her business would be the worst parts of my night. I'd been wrong. Harlow being upset was by far the worst.

"You don't need to worry about me. I'm fine. I just needed to get away and rest."

I brushed the hair that had fallen from her topknot out of her face. "I love you," I told her.

"I love you, too."

But I knew that wasn't enough. I had to prove to her just how much.

My sweet Lila Kate,

I've bought you more clothes than you'll ever wear. I've folded them and refolded them a million times. I keep making sure your little dresses are hanging properly in your closet and that you have shoes to match every outfit. Silly things that a baby wouldn't care about. But it gives me something to do while I wait for you.

I'm also making you a scrapbook with pictures of your daddy and me. There are even some with the three of us. I love the one where your daddy has his hand resting on my stomach. It's like he's holding you, too. Your daddy hired a photographer to come to the house and take photos of us yesterday—a surprise for me. We now have the most wonderful family photos in all my favorite parts of the house.

Actually, the swing under the tree is my favorite part of the house, and I can say I got to swing you on it first. I have photographic proof of that, too. It's the picture on the cover of your scrapbook. You'll recognize it right away.

One day, I imagine sitting outside with you on our porch and looking through this book. I expect it to be well worn with love over the years. You'll get to see just how much love you were brought into this world with.

But if I'm not there with you and you're looking through this scrapbook with your daddy or alone, know that I created each page with love. I was happier than I had ever been, and my life was complete.

Love you always,
Mommy

Harlow

I sealed the latest envelope and wrapped the thick stack of letters in a pink satin ribbon. I still had eight weeks of pregnancy left and would add more letters, but so far, I had written one to Lila Kate for each birthday and Christmas until she turned twenty-one, for her first day of kindergarten, her high school graduation, her wedding day, the birth of her first child, and her thirtieth birthday. Just in case I wasn't there, I wanted to leave a part of me with her. If I'd only had a part of my own mother growing up . . . I would have traded anything for it. At least Lila Kate would have that if she didn't have me.

I picked up the other stack of letters I had written. They were all to Grant: one for the day after my funeral, one for his first day alone with Lila Kate after everyone resumed normal life, one for her first day of kindergarten, and one in case he met a woman he could fall in love with. I wrapped those letters up with a red satin ribbon.

If I wasn't here to be his partner and help raise our little girl, I at least wanted my words to be there for him. I wanted him to know I was watching from above, that I was proud of him, and that I thought he was doing a wonderful job. I also wanted him to feel free to move on when the time came. He was my one and only love. He was my fairy tale. But it was possible I wouldn't be his. He had a long life ahead of him, and I didn't want him to spend it without someone by his side.

I placed both stacks of letters in the bottom drawer of Lila Kate's dresser. On top of both piles, I left one letter loose: the first one he would read. I would tell him that they were there when I felt it was time.

I left the scrapbook lying on the top of the dresser because Grant knew about it. He didn't know the real reason I wanted all those photos; he just knew I was making a scrapbook of memories for Lila Kate. I had framed my favorite photo of us sitting on the steps of the front porch. My head rested on Grant's shoulder, and his arm was wrapped around me, his hand splayed out over my stomach. It now hung over Lila Kate's changing table; you could see it the moment you walked into her room.

"You refolding baby clothes again?" Grant asked as he stepped into the room.

I laughed. He had caught me more than once reorganizing her closet and drawers. He didn't understand it, but he never teased me. He always smiled and told me Lila Kate was going to have the best mother in the world. I really hoped that was true.

Grant never spoke about what could happen. With each doctor's visit that went well—we continued to get good reports—he seemed less worried. He didn't stare at my stomach as if he was unsure about it anymore. As if it was the enemy. He touched it often, and he had even started talking to her.

"I want everything perfect for her," I told him, closing the drawer with the letters.

"It will be, because you'll be there," he replied.

Before I could say anything, he took a step toward me. "The photographer is coming back this afternoon. I have a few more pictures I'd like him to take."

He did? I had started to ask him about it when he stepped in front of me and took both of my hands. Then, as if in slow motion, he got down on one knee. All ability to speak or breathe left me. I wasn't expecting this. I had come to terms with the fact that he wasn't ready for marriage after the ball. Grant had already taken a huge chance on me. He didn't like taking chances. He was cautious.

"Harlow Manning," he said as he pulled out a black satin box from his pocket. "I think it's possible I fell in love with you the moment I laid eyes on you. I couldn't forget you. I looked for reasons to be around you. I dreamed and fantasized about you. Then somehow, over Chinese takeout, I managed to get you to sit in the same room with me for longer than a minute. I knew that night when I kissed you that I'd never be the same. Nothing would. You had marked my life."

He swallowed hard and gave me a shaky smile as he flipped open the box. A teardrop diamond was nestled in a small velvet cushion. It was simple and elegant. It was perfect. I didn't wear jewelry often, but this . . . this I would wear forever. My eyes were filling with tears and blurring my vision. This was really happening. I reached up to wipe the tears that had escaped and let out a soft laugh at the emotional mess I had become.

"You terrify me. Nothing in this world has ever shone as brightly as you do or made me want to be a better person like you do. I'll spend a lifetime trying to be worthy of you, but

I won't be. No one could ever be. You're a rare and precious gift, and I can't imagine my life without you in it, by my side. You're my happiness. You're my home. Will you make me the luckiest man alive and be my wife?"

Tears were freely streaming down my face now as I stood there with this beautiful man on his knees in front of me. A man who had just said such heartbreakingly sweet words to me. "Yes," I said, unable to say anything else. I didn't have to remind him of the chance he was taking. He knew. We both knew. He didn't care. I was worth taking a chance for. That was what he was telling me.

"Yes?" he repeated, grinning up at me.

I nodded my head, and he let out a relieved laugh, then shot to his feet and grabbed my face with his hands. His lips covered mine, and I knew that if I died tomorrow, I had lived. I had lived big.

Grant picked me up and started carrying me out of the room.

"Put me down, I weigh a ton!" I said, worried he was going to hurt his back.

"You've gained eighteen pounds, baby. That's not a ton."

He was headed for our bedroom, and I decided that arguing with him might not be to my advantage. If this was going where I thought it was, I was completely on board. Grant laid me down carefully on the bed and bent down to slip my shoes off. He kissed the arches of both feet before standing up and taking my shirt off. I let him undress me like I was helpless, because he seemed to be enjoying himself. When he tugged on my leggings, I lifted my bottom so he could slip them off, leaving me completely naked and him fully clothed.

"This is slightly unfair," I said, reaching for the button on his jeans. He chuckled and let me unsnap them. Then he discarded them, followed by his shirt. I took in his firm, sculpted body and lifted a hand to run it over his stomach. I loved the way it felt, and when he flexed, it was even better.

"Lie back and spread those legs open for me." His voice dropped to a sexy, husky sound, and his eyelids dropped as his gaze traveled down my body. I scooted back and opened my legs as instructed. Watching Grant's sexy smirk before he lowered his head between my legs made me shiver in anticipation. I loved the way he made me feel.

When his tongue took a swipe up through my slit, I reached up and grabbed the headboard in an attempt not to grab his hair and take or lose control. Whichever. I was more sensitive down there than I had ever been, but I had read that this was normal. I thought about sex a lot more than I used to. Although looking at Grant often made my mind go to sex. Sweaty, hot, wild sex. The kind we currently couldn't have. I wanted it, though. I wanted it bad.

"Give me your hand," he ordered, and I quickly obeyed. He moved it over my wetness. "Hold it open while I lick."

Oh, my. This was new. I reached down and used both hands to hold open my folds while he licked from my tingling spot, which was so close to an orgasm, to my opening, which was contracting in anticipation of being filled. I started to cry out as the orgasm grew, but right before it flung me over the cliff, he stopped, and his body moved up over mine. He slid inside me, slow and easy, as a growl of approval tore from his chest.

"I swear, every time I'm inside you, I think it's the absolutely best fucking feeling in the world, but each time, it's even better." I clawed at his back, and he began to move faster. "Never can get enough of you. I want to live inside this pussy," he said as my orgasm once again reached its crest. Instead of pulling away this time, his mouth lowered and clamped down on one of my nipples as the waves broke free, sending me spiraling into wonderland.

"Fuck, yes, that's sexy as hell," he said as his hips jerked faster, and my name tore from his chest in a growl before he rolled over, carrying me with him so that he stayed inside me but I was on top.

"Can't stop," he said, gasping. "Coming now." He jerked again, and his body shuddered.

When he was finished, I kissed a trail from his shoulder to his mouth.

"When it's safe again, I've got plans for you, sweet girl. Dirty, naughty plans."

"Is that a promise?" I asked, smiling down at him.

"Hell, yeah, it is," he replied.

⌗

Late that night, after hours of Grant showing me just how much he loved me and feeling every pleasure he could provide, a sharp pain hit me. Soon I was curled up in a ball and screaming. The pain was too much, and I knew it couldn't be right. I had read all about contractions. Something was wrong. Very wrong.

Grant jumped out of bed, trying to talk to me, but I couldn't make out the words or respond. I was doing all I could to keep from crying out in pain again. His voice didn't soothe me. Nothing helped. The pain slowly started to fade and then hit again.

"Ambulance will be here in five minutes." Grant's voice was filled with pure terror. I wanted to comfort him, but this time, I couldn't. I had to take care of me and our baby. A cool, damp cloth touched my forehead as he told me how much he loved me and how he was going to take care of me. Then he cursed and felt the warmth between my legs.

"God, no. Fuck!"

I glanced down, and all I saw was blood. And then it all went black.

Grant

The doors swung closed behind the doctor and nurses who surrounded Harlow as they wheeled her unconscious body on a gurney away from me. They wouldn't let me go any farther. I was numb with pain and terror. My life had just rolled away behind those doors, with no promise of return.

I stared through the small windows of the doors and watched the gurney disappear around a corner. I had to wait here. That was all they had said. Nothing more. They didn't tell me if I would see Harlow's smile again. They didn't tell me if she'd ever open her eyes again. And they didn't tell me if Lila Kate was ever going to see this world.

I knew nothing except that my heart and soul were back there somewhere with Harlow.

"Grant." Rush's voice called out to me, but I didn't turn around. I kept my eyes trained on that window. It was my only connection to where they had taken Harlow. Arms wrapped around me, and one large hand rested on my shoulder. I hadn't called anyone. I didn't know how Blaire and Rush even knew. If I could speak, I'd ask them, but I wasn't able to do that just yet. I was scared to do anything. I needed to focus on this door. *I have to will her to live for me. To come back to me.*

"Bethy saw the ambulance leaving your house on her way home from work. She called us," Blaire said, without my having to ask. "She's with Nate now. Woods and Della are on their way, and Rush is going to call Mase now. We thought we'd let him call Kiro." Out of the corner of my eye, I saw Rush nod, then head off to make the call.

Kiro. That was my one reprieve. I wouldn't have to live without Harlow, because if she didn't make it, Kiro was going to take my life, too. I would hand him my gun if he wanted it.

"Do we know anything?" Della asked as I heard footsteps running toward us. I didn't look at her. I had to keep watching these doors. This window.

"No. Rush just went to call Mase. I was going to have him ask. I figured he could get someone to talk."

"Woods will do it," Della said.

I felt a squeeze on my shoulder. "I'll be right back," Woods said. "We're here, man. It's gonna be OK. She's a fighter."

I managed what I thought was a nod or something close. Because I wasn't sure it would be OK. I wasn't sure if anything would ever be OK again.

"Mase is on his way," Rush said, walking up to stand beside me. "This place is about to be full of people. I'm sorry, but they all love you and Harlow. She's a part of us now."

She was the best part. But I didn't say that.

After a gentle squeeze of my arm, Blaire finally let go of her hold on me. "Come sit down," she said gently.

"No. I have to see." I wasn't going to explain more than that. I just wasn't moving from this spot.

"Y'all go have a seat. I'll stay here with him," Rush said, seeming to understand my need to watch out for her.

The crowd slowly moved away, but Rush remained by my side. I wouldn't tell him this, but I needed him. Just having him there beside me helped. I felt stronger. I felt like I might not shatter into a million pieces while waiting for Harlow if I had him there, helping me hold it together.

I hadn't bothered with calling my dad. He hadn't asked me about Harlow since that phone call months ago. He didn't bother to care what I was doing with my life. He just cared about me doing my job. Eventually, I would have to call him. He'd have to know why I wasn't going to work.

"She's in surgery. That's all I got. They will let us know more soon," Woods said.

She was in surgery. I wasn't there to hold her hand. I wasn't there to tell her she was going to be OK. She was alone. She needed me.

"She needs me," I choked out.

"She needs you to be strong. That's what she needs," Rush said.

I knew that, but I wasn't sure how strong I could be, imagining her on a table being cut open. What if they made a mistake? What if her heart couldn't handle it?

"When we were kids, she had open-heart surgery. She was so damn scared. She curled up in Kiro's lap the night before, and he told her a story about a princess who went to sleep. All she needed to wake up was the man who loved her most to be there waiting for her. And if she knew he was there, she'd wake up to see him." Rush let out a soft chuckle. "I thought it was a silly story then, but after the surgery, when I was finally able to see her, Dad took me back to her room. I asked her about being put to sleep and if it was as scary as she thought. She shook her head and said, 'No. I knew my daddy was here waiting for me to wake up. So I did.' And it was that simple. She knows you're waiting for her to wake up. I have faith she'll do it."

I wanted to believe I was her strength. That she'd come back for me. That she wouldn't give up. But right now, I was so scared that my hope wasn't enough. I kept seeing all that blood on the bed and her face go so pale, and then she was out. Nothing. Her heart had been beating, and she had been breathing, but mine had stopped. It was my worst nightmare come to life.

I heard more voices fill the waiting room behind me, but I didn't move or look back at them. Rush stood dutifully at my side, and we remained silent. I watched that door, and I think he did, too.

Nurses came and went through the double doors. One stopped and asked us what we were doing, and Rush explained that we were waiting. She must have seen the determined look on my face, because she didn't argue. She just walked away.

Several people came up to me to pat me on the back and offer their support. Jimmy, Thad, Bethy's aunt Darla, and even Henry, the valet kid. I wasn't sure who all else had arrived. I wasn't turning my eyes away even for a moment.

"Have you heard anything?" Nan's voice surprised me, and I tensed. Right now was not a good time for her to show up. I wanted her to leave. She didn't care about Harlow. She had never been kind to Harlow. She had made Harlow's life hell every chance she got.

"No. If you're gonna stay, go sit down in the waiting area with everyone else," Rush told his sister.

I expected her to argue or say something snide. But she didn't. She just walked off. If my mind hadn't been completely focused on Harlow, I would wonder what the hell had just happened.

"You've been standing here for more than an hour. Can I get you a drink?" Rush asked.

"No." I wasn't fucking drinking a soda while Harlow's life hung in the balance.

"Fine. Dehydrate," he replied.

The doors swung open, and a doctor stepped out, scanning the area. His eyes landed on me. "I'm looking for the family of Harlow Manning," he said.

I tried to say I was the family, but nothing came out. Panic squeezed my throat so tightly I couldn't even breathe. This was it. This was my news.

"That would be us," Rush said when he realized I wasn't going to be able to do it.

The doctor walked over to us and glanced back over Rush's shoulder. "Haven't ever seen this waiting room quite so full," he said.

"Harlow's loved," Rush replied.

I managed to gasp in some air, and the doctor's eyes swung to me. "You OK?"

"He needs to know how Harlow is. He's about to go into a full panic attack," Blaire's voice said behind me.

"I need immediate family," the doctor said.

"She's my fiancée," I finally managed to speak out.

The doctor nodded. "All right, then, good enough. I assume the baby is yours."

I nodded.

"Well, congratulations. You have a baby girl born at two forty-five a.m. It's too early, but we had to do an emergency C-section. She will have to stay in NICU for a little while, but she is completely developed, and her heart looks good. She's three pounds ten ounces and sixteen inches long. I'll need you to fill out her birth certificate when you're ready to step back there and see her."

Lila Kate was alive. She was here. On September 28, 2014, I had become a dad. I sucked in a deep breath. Harlow had done it. She'd brought our baby into this world healthy and alive. But what about Harlow . . .

As if reading my thoughts, the doctor went on. "We lost Harlow for a couple of seconds. She came back fast, though. She's a fighter."

"You lost her?" I asked, not understanding what he was telling me.

"Her heart stopped beating, but she came back with a little help. However, she hasn't woken up and is in critical condition. I can't tell you right now if and when she'll wake up. Her heart and body suffered through a severe traumatic episode. She's lost a lot of blood, and she's going to need a transfusion. Because of her delicate nature, it needs to be A-positive. If there's a relative handy with her blood type, a parent or sibling, that would be best."

I was B-positive. I couldn't help her. She needed me, and I couldn't do anything.

"I'm O-negative," Woods said, stepping up beside me. "I'm not related, but I know O-negative is a universal donor."

The doctor nodded. "Yes, but if we had a family member with the same blood type, it would be best. If not, we will gladly take your offer."

"I'm A-positive. I'm her sister. I'll do it."

At Nan's words, the entire waiting room went silent.

My sweet Lila Kate,

Today you entered this world. I'm writing this before I've actually seen you. This is my letter to you if I'm not there to hold you and welcome you into this life. I can imagine, though, how perfect and beautiful you are. I bet you have your daddy's blue eyes. I hope you have his smile. He has a wonderful smile.

If you never got a chance to meet me, know that you were my greatest accomplishment. You were a dream that I never imagined would come true. Since I was a little girl, I wanted to be a mommy. I wanted a baby of my own. I didn't understand what that meant until I was told you were inside of me. I already loved your daddy so fiercely. You were a part of him, and I loved you with the same fierce adoration.

Every choice I made until this day has been one I wanted to make, and I wouldn't change a thing. I would love the chance to at least hold you, but if that doesn't happen, know that I held you inside of me for nine months (I hope) and cherished every day.

Sleep tight in the secure arms of your daddy. I know I have. He'll be good at making you feel safe. When you're scared, let him remind you that he's right there, always ready to hold you when you need it.

*More than anything, I want to tell you this: You are a
fighter. You are strong. You are brave. You can accomplish
anything you set your mind to. This world is yours to
make the most of, and I believe you will live a life so full of
happiness that I will feel it from above.*

*Never let others bring you down. Their words don't
change who you are. You are in control of who you are.
You, my sweet Lila Kate, are your mother's daughter. We
fight for what we want and what we believe in. We don't
listen to others, and we are secure in who we are. Show
the world how amazing Lila Kate Carter is, and climb
mountains, baby girl. Climb them all.*

Love you always,
Mommy

Grant

She was tiny. The most tiny, perfect thing I'd ever seen. They had made me wash up in a shower and put on scrubs before I walked into the small room where they were keeping Lila Kate. She was asleep inside an incubator, and there was a wire taped to her chest. Her little feet were drawn up close to her body. Besides a pair of tiny socks, she had on only a diaper and a little knit hat. Was she cold?

"In a couple of days, you can hold her. Right now, we need to monitor her and make sure she's as healthy as she appears to be. She came out with a loud battle cry, which is a very good sign," the nurse beside me said.

"She's tough. Like her mom," I replied, and my voice cracked.

They hadn't let me see Harlow yet. When they told me I could come back and see Lila Kate, I hadn't been sure I wanted to do that. Not without Harlow. She hadn't seen her yet. But the idea of Lila Kate lying back here alone without her mother was more than I could handle. Harlow would want me back here with our daughter. I wasn't going to let her down.

"You probably already know this, but she weighs three pounds ten ounces, which is good. There are some milestones she must reach before she can be released from NICU. Normally, for a baby born two months early, it can take a couple of weeks to reach those."

I wasn't ready to take her home. She was so tiny. I was afraid to hold her. She looked breakable. I needed Harlow for this. She'd know what to do. She'd hold her and reassure her and do all those things.

"If you want to sit in the rocking chair over there and watch her, you can. She may wake up soon, and then you can meet your daughter."

My daughter. I had a daughter. This little life was really a part of me. A part of Harlow. A sudden rush came over me, and I realized I loved this baby. I loved this baby completely. I adored her, and I didn't even know her. She was ours.

"I want to stay, but the moment I'm allowed to see Harlow, I want someone to come get me. Immediately," I stressed. She needed to hear my voice. She'd open her eyes when she heard my voice, and she'd know I was waiting for her. She had to. Lila Kate and I couldn't do this without her. They just needed to let me back there to see her. She was waiting for me. I knew she was.

I sat down in the rocking chair directly across from where Lila Kate had her head turned. When she woke up, I would see her little eyes. I couldn't tell who she looked like right now. She was so tiny she looked more like a baby doll than anything else.

Harlow had bought her an outfit to wear home from the hospital even before we knew if she was a boy or a girl. She had bought one for each gender, just in case. The little pink gown was packed in the hospital bag she had so lovingly prepared and left sitting on the changing table in the nursery. I was supposed to grab it when she went into labor, but things hadn't happened the way we'd planned. My only goal at the time was to get Harlow to the hospital. I would have to send Blaire to the house to get what we needed. I wasn't leaving this place. Not without my girls. Both of them.

Her little eyes fluttered and opened, and soon my daughter was staring straight at me. I stood up slowly, afraid I would startle her, and walked over to the incubator. I had been given gloves, and there were holes in the incubator so that I could reach in and touch her. When I stood over her, she followed my every move. I could almost see the curiosity in her little face.

"Hello, Lila Kate. It's me, your daddy. We've spoken before but not face-to-face like this," I told her as I eased a hand inside and touched her small hand with mine.

Tiny fingers wrapped around one of mine and held on as she continued to stare up at me. She needed me. That fact gripped me, and I wasn't sure if I was terrified or humbled.

"You're beautiful, just like your mommy. You'll get to see her soon. We're just waiting for her to wake up. We need her to wake up. She knows that. I'm gonna go tell her as soon as they'll let me."

The thumb of her other hand went straight to her mouth as she continued to gaze up at me. "You like that thumb, don't you? Your mommy and I watched you do that when you were inside her. We got to see you kick and move around and suck that thumb on a screen. The doctor warned us you'd probably be a thumb sucker."

She eased her grip on my finger, only to tighten it again. It was amazing how someone so small could hold on so tight.

"You'll be out of this box soon, and then I can show you the world. We can show you. Your mommy and me. Your mommy has your room decorated for you. She's spent a lot of time and love preparing it for your arrival. I look forward to the day the three of us walk into it together."

Lila Kate blinked her eyes and continued to watch me as she sucked away on her thumb. Her little legs stretched out and bounced right back, like they were on a spring. I put my other arm in the other hole and took one of her little socked feet and removed the sock so I could look at her toes. They were short and, like the rest of her, perfectly proportioned. I held her little foot in my hand as she kicked and squirmed. It was smaller than my finger. Only half the length.

Once I was done examining her feet, I put her sock back on. She didn't appear to be happy about it, because the kicking started up again with full force.

"Mr. Carter, Harlow's father has arrived. Mr. Finlay said to come get you."

Kiro was here. Time to face him. I understood his desire to kill me. Harlow was his world. She was a part of Emily, and the love he had for Emily spilled over onto Harlow. I understood that completely. Looking down at my own daughter, all I could see was her mother. In that moment, I learned that my heart was big enough to have two epic loves in my life.

"I'll be back. I have to go deal with your grandfather. You'll meet him soon enough. Prepare yourself. He's a lot to take in," I told her before pulling my hand out of the incubator, blowing her a kiss, and turning to leave.

I stopped at the door and looked at the nurse. "I'll be back. I don't want her left alone. Make sure she's warm enough."

The nurse smiled and nodded. "Yes, Mr. Carter. We will take care of her."

"Thanks," I replied, and headed to the waiting room.

I took the elevator back down to the waiting room and went to the closest nurses' station before going back out there and talking to Kiro.

"Is there any new information on Harlow Manning? Her sister was here to give blood for the transfusion she needed. I want an update."

The nurse nodded and picked up the phone. She spoke to the person on the other line, asked them about Harlow, then hung up and looked at me. "Are you her fiancé, Grant Carter?" the lady asked.

I nodded.

"The blood transfusion was successful. Harlow still hasn't opened her eyes. Her brain waves are positive, though. But until she opens her eyes, we can't be sure how much she was affected. A doctor will be out to speak with you shortly. They've gotten word that her father has arrived."

"Thanks," I said, holding on to the good news. I needed positive. I also didn't care if Kiro being here made them more anxious to answer my questions. If Kiro Manning made them jump, then good. I needed them to fucking jump. I didn't care how it happened.

The fact Nan had offered to give them the blood Harlow needed was still something I couldn't process. What did she have to gain by doing that? Nan never gave freely without trying to manipulate people. There had to be a reason she did it. But I honestly didn't care. She did it, and that was all that mattered.

Kiro

Why couldn't it have been *my* motherfucking heart? Why did it have to be my baby girl's? I had been asking this question since the day they told Emmy and me there was an issue with Harlow's heart. I would have moved heaven and earth to take that from her. But just like I couldn't save my Emmy, I couldn't save our daughter.

She was stubborn, and she was so fucking brave. That damn hard head of hers had been something I admired. Until she decided she was gonna have a baby. I knew she'd never abort it. Wasn't in her nature. She had been trying to save the world since she was three years old. She always put others before herself. She preferred the people she loved over her own wants and needs.

It was one of the things that made her so damn beautiful. Just like my Emmy. And she was all I had of my Emmy. The light in Emmy's eyes had been gone for so long. Every day I visited her, I hoped to see her eyes light up with understanding and that she would come back to me, but that never happened. Not once.

The only way I could see that light was to look at our Harlow. Our little miracle. And now she was lying back there on some goddamn hospital bed with tubes in her, barely hanging on to life.

All I could think about on the flight to Rosemary Beach was how I was going to wrap my hands around Grant Carter's neck for doing this to her. He hadn't thought about her safety; he had thought with his fucking dick. And my sweet Harlow loved the man. She wanted his kid. And he let her go through with it.

Now I was in the waiting room with everyone else. Rush tried to talk to me and calm me down. He didn't want me agitated when Grant came back from seeing the baby that might have just killed *my* baby. He said Grant was a wreck. That he had been standing there like a man possessed, watching the door for a sign of Harlow. For any word.

He was scared. Good. Motherfucking *good*! He should be. Maybe death was too good for him. A life like mine was hell on earth. That was what he deserved. Death would be too easy for him.

I glanced back at Dean, who was sitting with Blaire, then saw that the rest of the band had found places to sit. When I'd gotten the call, they had all shown up at the airport with me. They loved my girl, too. She was their family. There was a good chance they'd kill Grant.

"Kiro," Grant said, and I jerked my head back around to see the man responsible for this. He was wearing a pair of blue scrubs, and there were dark circles under his eyes. The pale color of his face didn't make me feel any better.

"You killed my baby," I snarled, unable not to take out my pain on someone.

Grant tensed, and Rush was there between us immediately. He looked fierce and ready to take me on.

"She's alive. She's fighting, because that's what she does. I don't give a damn who you are, I will have your ass removed from this hospital if you can't keep it together. I'm sorry you're hurting. I know you've got to be scared as shit. But so is he," Rush said, pointing at Grant. "He's fucking terrified. Losing her would destroy him. He's already breaking apart. So don't come in here throwing shit around and accusing him of anything. He stood by the woman he loves when she was determined to have this baby. He couldn't force her to do something she'd never get over."

Dean came up beside his son and put a hand on Rush's shoulder as if to make sure I knew I wasn't going to be able to attack Rush, either. "The boy looks like he's been through hell. Harlow wouldn't want this. She would want you to be here for each other. You know that, Kiro," Dean said in a stern tone.

They were all on the boy's side. He could have stopped this. My baby had wanted to give him a baby. She loved that baby because it was his. So hell, yes, I blamed him.

"He didn't protect her. He could have saved us all this with something as simple as a damn condom."

Grant closed his eyes, and I saw him tremble. Apparently, he knew that, too. He was taking the blame. Good. He needed to know that if we lost her, he was the one who killed her. Him.

"He didn't know about her heart until the day she left him. She was pregnant before she left. She just didn't know it," Rush explained.

I already knew that. I didn't care. He still should have used a condom. Respect a girl like Harlow, and protect her from your dick. It's fucking courtesy.

"Where the fuck is Mase? His ass should be here," I said, angry that the brother she adored wasn't here, waiting.

"I'm right here, asshole."

Mase

"You did not just call him an asshole," Major whispered beside me.

"Watch your mouth," my mother scolded. Although she knew he was an asshole.

"He is an asshole," I replied as I glared at the man who had a part in bringing me into this world. I wouldn't consider him a father. He was Harlow's father, not mine. And definitely not Nan's. He hadn't even claimed her until she was an adult, and only after Blaire's father shared that info with the world.

"He's Kiro. You can't call him an asshole," Major said.

Major hadn't grown up around that part of my life. His father was my stepdad's brother. I was kept away from Kiro's life as much as possible. Major had traveled the world as an army brat and only knew of Kiro Manning the rock god. He didn't know what a sucky excuse for a father he was.

"Your sister is in there dying, and the brother she fucking worships can't find it in his cowboy schedule to get his sorry ass over here fast enough. So who's the asshole?" Kiro spat back at me.

My mother tensed beside me and started off after him, but I grabbed her arm. She and Kiro didn't get along. He had been

188

a very bad mistake during a rebellious time in her life. I still can't figure out how she had gone that far off the deep end. But whenever I asked her about it, she would tell me it was Kiro Manning, and she had been a young girl. It was as simple as that. Then she'd remind me that she had me, which made it all worth it.

"I don't own my own fucking jet. I had to fly commercial. I got here as fast as I could. Look at me. I'm covered in dirt, sweat, and cow shit. I didn't even stop in the house to change. I ran for the motherfucking airport."

My mother didn't even try to correct my language this time.

Kiro looked somewhat appeased. He swung his gaze to Major and frowned. "Who the fuck is he?" he asked. He still hadn't acknowledged my mother. Asshole.

"Major Colt. My cousin. Major, this is Kiro Manning." I didn't add that he was my father. Major knew it, and I didn't like to remind myself or claim him as such. I put up with him because of Harlow. She was the only Manning I cared to have anything to do with. She was my little sister, and if Grant Carter didn't look completely fucked up right now, I'd beat the shit out of him. I needed to hit someone, and he was the only one I could think of to blame.

"You don't have any cousins. Your last name isn't Colt," Kiro said in that haughty tone of his that I hated. The rock star didn't affect me. That persona got to most people. But not his offspring. We knew better.

"Should have been," my mother snapped, and Kiro shifted his angry glare to her. I wouldn't let him speak down to her. I'd knock his old ass out if I had to.

"My last name is Colt-Manning. The man who raised me

is a Colt," I informed him. Kiro knew good and well that I was more a Colt than a Manning. A father was the man who was there for you, not the man who donated his sperm for the cause.

Kiro rolled his eyes and then stretched his neck by moving it from side to side. He was scared, and he was being a jerk in order not to beat the shit out of Grant. I could read him well enough to know why he was showing his worst side.

"I'm going to have a seat," my mother said, wanting to put distance between herself and Kiro.

I nodded and watched her walk over, take a seat, and pull out her phone to call home.

"It's a family gathering, I see," a female voice said, one I had hoped I'd never have to hear again.

I turned toward Nan. Why was she even here? She didn't care about Harlow. If she wasn't a damn female, I'd punch her to get some release—and pay her back for all the hurt she'd caused Harlow.

"Didn't expect you to be here," I said, not even trying to hide the distaste in my tone.

She shrugged and flipped her long red hair back over her shoulder. "We all share the same daddy," she said in a saccharine-sweet voice.

"Didn't fucking mean anything to you before. If you're here to move in on Grant, you can hang that idea up. In case you haven't noticed, he's falling apart. You're not even on his radar."

Nan flinched but only barely. I would have missed it had I not been watching her.

"Ease off," Rush warned. "She stepped in and volunteered to give blood when Harlow needed a transfusion. She doesn't deserve this from you."

Nan had given Harlow blood? For fucking real?

"What? Are you shitting me?" I asked, looking from Rush to Kiro, who looked equally shocked.

"Don't," Nan told Rush. "I didn't do it for his acceptance," she said, then spun around and stalked off.

Rush watched the sister we shared walk off with concern on his face. He had grown up with Nan. They'd been raised by the same selfish, shitty mom. Rush was the only person who loved Nan, and I respected that, but he overlooked a lot from her.

"Since she was ten years old, I haven't seen her do anything for anyone but herself. I haven't seen her show compassion or concern for anyone. I haven't seen her attempt to show others that she has a heart under all that bitterness. Until today. She didn't even hesitate. The doctor said they needed Harlow's blood type, and it would be best coming from a family member. Nan stood up and offered without a second thought."

That didn't make sense. That wasn't Nan. She didn't give without trying to manipulate something or someone. But right now, I didn't care. She had helped Harlow when she needed it most. I could forgive a lot for that.

Rush turned and walked over to Blaire, and Kiro went to lean against the nearest wall. I turned to look for Grant and found him standing with his arms crossed over his chest as he watched the two double doors the doctor had gone through as if he was waiting for him to return.

"OK, the redhead is your sister, too? Damn, she's hot. How many hot sisters do you have, and how the hell didn't I know about that one?"

I ignored Major. He didn't know Nan. He had no idea what she was like. If he was smart, he never would. He'd go back to Texas and forget about my other sister. I had.

Grant

Two days later

"Mr. Carter?" a voice said as a hand touched my arm and shook it. My eyes snapped open, and I blinked, looking up at the nurse standing over me. "I'm sorry to wake you, but the doctor just came in and checked on Lila Kate. You've been cleared to hold her if you're ready."

Hold her. I had watched over her for two days while waiting for them to tell me I could see Harlow.

"Harlow? Can I see her?" I wanted to see Harlow first. I wanted to tell her about Lila Kate. I also wanted her to wake up and be there when I held the baby for the first time. I didn't want to do that without Harlow.

The nurse smiled. "Actually, that's the other thing I was going to tell you. She's stable, and although she still hasn't opened her eyes, it's safe for you to see her. Her cardiologist said she'd want to see you before her father. He thinks your voice will give her something to fight for."

I glanced over at my sleeping daughter. I was ready to hold her. She'd been holding my finger and staring at me as I talked to her continually. She was a good baby, the nurses said. She didn't cry a lot, but when she did cry, she raised hell. Which only made me smile.

"I want to see Harlow first," I told the nurse, and she nodded and opened the door.

"Let's go, then."

I started to follow her, then stopped. I turned back and walked over to Lila Kate. I reached inside and rubbed her little sleeping face. "I'm going to see Mommy now. Wish me luck," I whispered.

When I finally followed the nurse out the door, I noticed she had watery eyes. If she only knew. I had two angels in this world, and I would do anything to save them both. I wanted that life Harlow and I had planned and dreamed about. She just had to wake up.

"You need to be prepared before you go in there. She's hooked up to a few machines. We were able to take off the oxygen mask; she's doing so well that we aren't worried about her breathing purified air. But she still has a feeding tube in her throat. Just know that's food, not oxygen. There are dark circles under her eyes, and she's lost some weight. Just know she's doing better than expected after what she went through. Most women don't survive that."

When the door opened, the pain in my chest felt like an explosion. She was so helpless, and she seemed so small on that hospital bed. She had been alone in here without me for almost three days. I hated not being able to be with her. It made me physically ill to think she might believe I'd abandoned her.

"I'll be right outside the door if you need me," the nurse said before closing it.

I walked over to the side of the bed and touched her hand. It was cool. It needed my warmth. "Hey, sweet girl. I'm here. I've been waiting for them to tell me I could come see you. I've been telling Lila Kate all about you. She's ready to see her mommy. I think I have someone who understands just how much I love you now, because it's obvious she does, too," I said, trying my hardest not to crack.

I didn't want her upset. I wanted to sound upbeat and give her strength. I wanted her to know I believed she could pull out of this.

"You have a waiting room full of people who love you. Rush and Blaire have been here since moments after they rolled you away from me. Nate's even stopped by to visit everyone. Della and Woods and Mase are here. Mase even brought Major with him. And your dad is here, along with the entire band. It's causing some excitement in the hospital. Having every member of Slacker Demon hanging out in the waiting room and ordering pizza is more excitement than this place has seen in a while."

I was rambling now. I just wanted her to know how loved she was. I didn't want her to think we didn't need her. Because we did. I did. Lila Kate did.

"Lila Kate is beautiful. She's perfect. I can't wait until you can hold her. They told me before I came in here that I can hold her now. She's been holding on to my finger the past couple of days. She's tiny, and they had to put her in an incubator, but she's not having any complications. She's progressing well. And when I talk, she watches me so closely. But I think she's looking for you. She's waiting for her mommy to show up. Oh, and she sucks her thumb like a champ. She loves that thumb. It's her favorite pastime. I know breaking her of it one day won't be easy, but right now, it's so damn cute I don't care."

I threaded her limp fingers through mine and held her hand tightly. Then I lifted it up and kissed it. I saw the bruises on her hands from being stuck with so many needles. I kissed each one, then held her hand to my lips. They weren't going to be able to force me from this spot. When I had watched her roll away, I thought I'd never touch her or hold her again. But she was here. And she was breathing, and she was going to come back to me.

"You gotta wake up for me, sweet girl. You gotta wake up for us. Lila Kate and I are waiting for you. We want to walk into her bedroom with you right there beside us. I'm not as strong as you, Harlow. I can't live without you. I can't fight like you can. I need you. I can't do this with Lila Kate alone. She needs you. She needs her mother. She needs what you didn't have. Fight, baby. Fight for her. Fight to open your eyes and come back to us. I believe in you. You showed me you could bring this precious baby girl into the world. Now show me you can stay with me. Show me." I stopped before I started begging.

There was a knock on the door, and a nurse stepped inside. "Mr. Manning is wanting to see her," she said. I could tell by the look on her face that Kiro was raising hell. I nodded and tuned back to Harlow.

"Your daddy is throwing a fit in the waiting room. He's worried about you. You've scared him good. I'm gonna step out and let him come visit you. I'll be back. I'm going to go tell Lila Kate about this and how good you look. I'm going to tell her to get ready. You'll be awake soon. And I'm going to hold her. I wanted to wait for you, but I don't want to make her wait to be held any longer. I'll rock her and tell you all about it when I come back."

I bent down and pressed a kiss to her dry lips. She would hate that her lips were dry.

I turned to the nurse. "Can you get her something for her lips? They're dry. That bothers her. It's uncomfortable for her."

The nurse nodded. "Yes, sir. We'll do that."

"I'll be back after her father and her brother visit her. I expect that you will have handled it by then."

She nodded. "Yes, we will do it right now."

I glanced back at Harlow one more time before stepping out of the room and heading back to the NICU.

My sweet Lila Kate,

Life in your beautiful room must make you feel like the princess you are. I know Daddy loves your sweet face and kisses it often. Smile for him. Give him a reason to smile again. If I'm not there with you, be his strength, and teach him that loving someone is a chance we all take, but life without love means nothing. If he didn't take a chance, he wouldn't have you in his arms right now.

I don't know if I'll get a chance to tell you this story in person, so I want to tell you now. It's one my daddy told me a long time ago. I held it close to me all my life, and it made me brave. It got me through some tough times, and I want you to understand how you play a really important part in this story.

Once upon a time, there was this princess. She was loved in her kingdom for her heart. They didn't care about her outer beauty. It was the inside that mattered to them. But one day, she was cursed by a very jealous evil queen. She was put into a deep sleep. To wake her up, the one man in all the world who loved her most had to be waiting for her. If she knew he was there waiting, she would open her eyes for him. But there's a part of that story that my daddy left out. A part I think is most important.

The man who loved her most in the world was there, but she didn't have to open her eyes, because she had left him a gift. A special, beautiful baby girl to love him and take care of him. A reason for him to live his life full of happiness. So there was no reason for the princess to open her eyes. She knew that if it was too hard to wake up, then she would be leaving behind love and joy instead of sadness.

If I'm reading this to you, the princess was able to open her eyes this time. But if I'm not, I know she left the man who loved her the most with someone he loved just as much.

Love you always,
Mommy

Grant

She needed me to hold her. She needed to know she was loved. But she was so small, and Harlow wasn't here to help me do this right. What if I did it wrong? I didn't want to hurt her.

"Just sit down in the rocker, and I'll bring her to you all bundled up in a blanket. You look nervous, but that's normal, especially for new daddies," the nurse said as she opened the incubator. Lila Kate started kicking happily, and her thumb came out of her mouth, as if she was ready for this and needed both hands.

The nurse changed her diaper, which also looked confusing as hell, then wrapped her up tight in a blanket. When she went to pick her up, I held my breath and jumped up to put my hands under hers in case she dropped my baby.

The nurse chuckled. "I won't drop her. I promise," she said, smiling at my sudden reaction to seeing Lila Kate moved from the safety of her box.

I forced myself to back up and sit down in the rocking chair.

"See how I'm holding her so I'm supporting her head? She needs that. She can't hold her head up by herself, so you support it with your arms and hold her close to you. She's a preemie and needs the warmth. She also needs the bonding. You've done a great job with her, sitting and letting her hold your finger, but she needs more than that now. You can hold her as long as you want. If you don't feel comfortable standing up with her, you can press that button on the wall beside you. and I'll walk you through it. But you've got to learn how to do this on your own."

I would be taking her home one day. The nurse didn't say that, but I knew that was what she meant. I hadn't allowed myself to imagine taking Lila Kate home without Harlow. It wasn't something I wanted to consider. Now there was a chance I would have to take our daughter home without her. I didn't want that. I wanted her mother with us. I wanted my family.

"You ready?" she asked.

I nodded. I had to be ready. I was Lila Kate's daddy.

She placed the little bundle in my arms, and her clean baby scent hit my nose. Her little eyes studied me as she gazed up at me.

"I'll leave you two alone. Buzz if you need me," the nurse said, then left us.

I cuddled her close to my chest, and it was amazing how little she weighed. She felt like a feather. Her small thumb found her mouth again.

"I just saw Mommy. She hasn't opened her eyes yet, but she's going to. She wants to, because she wants to see you so much. We just have to be patient. Give her time to heal. The first thing she's going to want to do is hold you. I better enjoy this now, because once she wakes up, she may never let you go. I can't wait to see my two favorite girls together. It'll be the prettiest picture in the world."

Lila Kate frowned and puckered up like she was about to cry. I wasn't sure what to do with crying babies, but it was time I figured it out. I pulled her up higher on my chest and tucked her toward me. Then we rocked.

The motion soothed her, and the puckered pre-cry look went away. Her little eyes started to slowly close.

And as if it was the most natural thing in the world, I sang to her. Every lullaby I could think of as I rocked her. Long after her little eyes closed and she turned her face to bury it in my chest, I continued to sing to her.

A knock on the door interrupted my singing, and I looked up as Blaire stuck her head in the room. She looked unsure, but she eyed Lila Kate like she wanted to get a hold of her. Too bad I wasn't handing her over.

"I brought the bags from the house Harlow had packed. I searched the drawers for anything smaller for Lila Kate to wear home, but there wasn't anything for preemies."

"She's wearing what Harlow bought her. It'll work. Harlow picked it out," I said.

She smiled. "Then she needs to wear what her mommy picked out. I did find something, though. Actually, a lot of somethings. I don't know if you know about them," Blaire said, holding up a sealed envelope. It was Harlow's stationery. I had seen her write on it many times. "There are a bunch of these, but this was the only loose one, and it was addressed to you, so I brought it. Maybe it wasn't meant for you to read yet, but with things like they are now, I think it might help you. I'll leave it here for you to read later." She stepped closer to peer down at Lila Kate. "She's perfect. Absolutely perfect."

I already knew that, but hearing her agree with me made my chest swell with pride. "She looks like her mother. She had no choice but to be perfect," I said, thinking of how I needed to get back to Harlow.

"Have Mase and Kiro seen Harlow?" I asked.

She nodded. "Mase is still in there. His mother is with him. She asked about Lila Kate, and I told her you were with her now. I think Harlow's important to her. Anyway, you may have to kick Mase out."

I was glad she wasn't alone. While I was with Lila Kate, I wanted someone to be with Harlow.

"Rush said you told the doctor Harlow was your fiancée. We weren't sure if you were just saying that or—"

"I proposed to her earlier in the evening the night this all happened. She said yes," I said, swallowing against the emotion that came from remembering Harlow's smile. She'd been so happy. I had been fucking thrilled. Then it had all gone to hell.

"Congratulations," Blaire said, smiling at me. "I was wondering when that was going to happen. I can't wait to see her ring and help her make plans." The one thing I loved about Blaire was that she didn't think the worst. She was positive. She believed in Harlow, too. I needed that right now.

"Thanks. I'm anxious to see it on her hand again," I said as I gazed down at the little girl in my arms. "I'm even more anxious to see Lila Kate in her arms."

"If you want to go back to Harlow, I'll hold Lila Kate and stay with her. I can rock her as long as you need me to. I won't leave her alone," Blaire offered.

I wanted to read that letter, and I wanted to get back to Harlow.

"OK, yeah, that would be great. I don't want to stick her back in that thing until they make me."

"I don't blame you. She's seen enough of that thing." Blaire reached for her, and I froze. She was standing up. I didn't want anyone to stand up and hold her. It was a long way to the floor.

"What's wrong?" Blaire asked.

"I'm, uh . . . I just . . . I don't want you to drop her."

Blaire's eyes went wide, then she broke out into a huge smile. "I think I can manage not to drop her. But if it makes you feel better, you can keep your hands under her until you feel safe. God knows Rush did that enough with Nate. I'm used to it."

She had successfully not dropped her kid for almost a year, so I decided to trust her. I handed Lila Kate over to her slowly and with extreme care. When I was sure she had a good hold on her, I moved my hands under her, then stood up slowly and stayed in the catch position until Blaire was sitting safely in the rocker.

"Success," Blaire said teasingly.

"Thanks for staying with her. I'll be back later. They may come in here and put her back in the incubator, but if you wouldn't mind sitting and watching her, I'd appreciate it. She likes to be talked to while she's in that thing."

Blaire nodded. "Got it. We will chat. I got this. Go on, Daddy."

I reached for the letter she had laid down when she walked in and headed out the door. I stopped to let the nurse know I'd left Lila Kate with her aunt, then headed for the elevators.

To the love of my life,

If you've found this letter, then I'm not at home with you and our little girl. I hope I've told you where to find all the letters I left behind, but if I didn't, I'm glad you found them now.

I know I told you I would make it and that I was strong enough. I was determined enough to get through this. I had hoped that if I believed it hard enough, I would be able to get through it.

Forgive me. I never wanted to leave you. I wanted that life we talked about. I wanted to hold our little girl and watch Lila Kate take her first steps with you. I wanted all those things. If you're reading this now, I didn't get those things, but I did have you.

I knew what it was like to be loved by you. My life may have been cut short, but in that life, I had the love of a man who made me feel special and cherished. I knew the joy of feeling his baby move inside of me. I was able to watch his face while he felt our little girl kick me and the moment he heard her heart beat the first time. The look on your face was one of those moments all women deserve. I got something that people spend their lives looking for. I couldn't have asked for more. You made every day new and exciting. Being with you made me feel safe and loved. Giving you the gift of our little girl was something I got to do.

Not having her was something I never considered. I couldn't. I loved her the moment I knew I was pregnant. She was us. And now that you can hold her and see her, you understand. How could I give her up to save myself?

You gave me the moments in life that are worth living for. You made my life this bright, shining, wonderful world. Thank you for that. Thank you for everything. I love you, Grant Carter. Every time you look into our daughter's face, know that I love you both.

There are more letters. The ones I haven't tied up yet are letters I wrote about our experience during my pregnancy, and they are all to Lila Kate. It tells her everything I was feeling, and I want you to read them to her when she's old enough to understand.

Then there's a stack of letters tied in a pink ribbon. Each is labeled. They're for specific events and moments in Lila Kate's life. She won't have me there, but she will have my love and my words.

The stack with a red ribbon is for you. They're also labeled. You'll know when you're supposed to open each one. Don't read them now. Give it time. Wait and read them when each letter is meant to be opened. It will be what you need to hear at that moment in time.

You were my world. You were my one and only. I left you, but I left another love behind. Never let a day go by that Lila Kate doesn't know how much you love her. Love her for me, too.

Forever and always,
Harlow

Grant

She had prepared letters in case she didn't make it. I leaned against the wall of an empty hallway in the hospital. My face was wet with tears, and I didn't give a shit. Each tear fell because I wasn't reading this for the reason she thought I'd be. She hadn't left us. She was here fighting hard to stay with us. When her heart had stopped, she hadn't let go.

She was my fighter. My beautiful, wonderful fighter.

I folded the letter and pressed a kiss to the paper, knowing she had held it not too long ago, then I tucked it into my pocket. I was going to tell her I didn't accept this. Because she was still here. She was still holding on, and it was time she opened those pretty hazel eyes and looked at me.

I wiped my face and headed for the ICU.

Once I got there, I saw Mase leaning against her door, his head hanging until his chin touched his chest. His shoulders were sagging, and he looked defeated. He needed to take his ass back to the waiting room if he was going to mope. She was going to wake up soon. He didn't need to act like she was gone. She wasn't gone.

I wasn't letting her go.

His head lifted when I stopped in front of him. He looked strangely hopeful.

Had something happened? Why was he outside her door instead of in the room with her?

"What are you doing out here?" I asked, not liking the idea of her being in there alone.

"She opened her eyes and said your name through the tube in her throat, then closed her eyes again."

His words took a moment to sink in. Then I shoved him out of my way and jerked the door open to see two nurses and a doctor standing over her. The feeding tube in her throat was gone, and so were several of the wires, but her eyes weren't open.

"Well, hello, Mr. Carter," the doctor said.

"She opened her eyes?" I asked, needing them to confirm.

"That's what Mr. Manning, the younger one, said. According to her chart, it looks like there's been some action. We took out the feeding tube because he said she tried to talk with it. Even said your name. Now we wait. If she's coming out of it, she's exhausted, and her body will only be able to stay awake for small amounts of time. But with the proper care, I believe Harlow is going to watch her little girl grow up. If we're lucky."

My knees buckled, and I had to grab the edge of the bed. The sob that broke free from me wasn't something I could control. "She's not leaving me," was all I could say.

The door opened, and Mase came in and looked at me, then at Harlow. "Is she OK?" he asked in a panic.

"Yes. Mr. Carter is just overcome with the news that his fiancée will be waking up for good soon."

"Thank God," Mase muttered, and sank into the nearest chair, dropping his head into his hands.

"Right now, she needs Grant to talk to her. I suspect she was trying to wake up for him, and I'm sure she wants to know about their baby girl. Let's give them some time alone," the doctor said as he opened the door and waited for Mase to stand up and follow.

Mase looked reluctant to leave. "Will you send word as soon as she's awake?" he asked me.

"Of course," I assured him.

He nodded, then followed the doctor out of the room.

I pulled a chair beside her bed and sat down. Her hand was still cool, so I pulled it between both of mine and warmed it.

"I wasn't here when you called for me. I was rocking Lila Kate. They let me hold her. She's as light as a feather, and she smells really good. I sang to her. I sang every lullaby I could think of, and then I just started singing her Toby Keith songs. I think she really likes 'I Love This Bar.'"

I took a deep breath. I wanted to see her eyes open so badly. It could be hours before she did it again. I had to be patient with her. Give her time.

"I read your letter. At least the first one. Blaire found the letters when she went to the house to get our things." I stopped and brought her hand to my mouth and kissed it. "I don't accept that. I mean, I accept the fact that I'm your world and your one and only, but I don't accept that I won't get forever with you. You opened your eyes before, and now you're going to open them again. And you're going to talk to me."

"'K." The word fell from her lips in a soft whisper, and my

heart leaped from my chest. Her hand moved in mine and gave me a gentle, weak squeeze.

"You're awake. You can hear me," I said, staring in awe at her.

"Mm-hmm," she said, still almost too softly. But I could hear her.

"Show me those eyes, sweet girl. I need to see those eyes."

Her eyelashes fluttered a little, and then, as if in slow motion, they opened, and it took a moment for her to focus, but when she did, she was looking directly at me.

I stood up and bent down over her, then pressed my forehead to hers. "You did it," I said before kissing her lips. They weren't dry this time. The nurse had done as I requested. "And she's the most perfect little girl in the world. I've told her all about you, and she's getting impatient to meet you."

A soft laugh escaped her mouth, and I took the first deep breath since she'd screamed out in pain in our bed.

"You laugh, but she's demanding for a four-pound baby, and I'm pretty sure she's already wrapped me around that tiny finger." I pulled back so I could look at her. "You scared me," I admitted.

She gave me a sad smile. "Sorry," she whispered.

I cupped her face. "You came back. That's all that matters. You didn't give up. You opened your eyes for me. For us. Because, let me tell you, Lila Kate and I need her mommy very much."

"See . . . her?" she asked, her whisper getting stronger.

"Wait right there. Keep those eyes open," I told her, and backed up to the door without taking my eyes off her.

She smiled at me, and I winked back.

Opening the door, I still didn't take my eyes off her. "She's awake and talking to me. She needs water, and we need our daughter. Someone make that happen," I called out to whoever was out there and could hear me.

A nurse ran up to the door immediately. I held Harlow's hand as the nurse checked her vitals.

"You decided to join us. You have three very anxious men and one little girl who were waiting not so patiently to see you."

Harlow looked at me. "Three?" she asked.

"Kiro and Mase and the rest of this town and every member of Slacker Demon. But yeah, your brother and dad are going to want to see you. They've been here the entire time. We had to force Mase to take a shower and change, because he showed up filthy and smelling bad after a middle-of-the-night emergency with a horse."

Harlow let out a soft laugh.

"I don't want to leave her. Can you send someone for her brother and dad?" I asked the nurse.

"Her doctor is on his way over right now and will want to check some things. We'll have to ask you to step out while he does that. If he gives her the all-clear, we can possibly move her to a wheelchair and pay a visit to your baby girl. But first, the doctor has to see her."

I wasn't OK with the leaving her part. I started to shake my head, but Harlow's hand squeezed mine firmer this time. "I won't leave again. I'm back. I will be here when you get back. I want to see Dad and Mase."

"Promise me," I said, still not sure I was ready to walk out of the room yet.

"I promise," she assured me.

With one last kiss to her head, I made my way back to the waiting room to tell them all that Harlow was awake. Then I went to talk to the nurses in the NICU to see if we could get Lila Kate to her mother sooner.

Harlow

"I'm sure your sister will want a chance to come back and see you, too. The men were just more demanding," the nurse said after Grant stepped out of the room.

My sister? Did she think Blaire was my sister?

"Considering she was the hero, I think she deserves first visit, but your dad and your brother may not let that happen."

"Hero?" I asked, not sure what she was talking about. Blaire had very likely done something while I was out that saved the day. I just didn't know what that was.

The nurse smiled at me as she adjusted something attached to me. "You lost a lot of blood, and you needed a transfusion. You not only don't have an easy blood type to match, but when someone with your condition needs blood, it's best to use a relative with the same blood type if at all possible. A parent or a sibling. Your sister jumped right up and offered. Made it happen much faster than if we'd had to seek a donor."

Nan? I couldn't imagine Nan would offer to give me a cup of water if I was on fire, much less blood. Was she even here?

"What sister?" I asked. My throat was sore and dry, and I was trying not to talk, but I had to know who she was talking about.

"You have more than one? I didn't realize that. The tall red-head. Gorgeous," she said.

It had been Nan. Oh, wow. Nan was here, and she'd given me blood. Maybe I was still asleep. Was this a dream? Was I not about to see my baby girl? Tears welled up in my eyes. I wanted to be awake. Lila Kate was waiting for me, and Grant needed me. He had been so pitiful, begging me to open my eyes. I had been fighting so hard to say something to ease his fears. I thought it had really happened.

"Why are you crying? Did I hurt you? Does something hurt?" The nurse looked panicked.

I shook my head and sniffed. At least, the nurse in my dream was kind. "I'm still asleep," I said as a sob broke free.

She frowned and had started to speak when the door opened and the doctor walked in. "Well, look who decided to join us." He beamed at me.

I cried harder. I so wanted to be awake.

"What's wrong?" the doctor asked.

"She thinks she's still asleep," the nurse explained.

"What? Why?"

The nurse shrugged and shook her head. "I have no idea."

"We don't want you crying. We want you smiling. You showed us all just how strong you are. No little heart disease is gonna keep you down. You get to see your baby girl soon. She's a beauty, let me tell you." He was trying to be jolly, but it wasn't helping.

"I'm still asleep. I want to see her, but I'm still asleep," I said as the tears continued to fall.

The doctor frowned and patted my arm. "No, Harlow,

you're awake, sweetheart. Very awake. You have a waiting room packed with people who just shouted out in a very loud cheer when Grant announced that you were awake and talking. I've never seen anything like it. Made my heart feel good. So stop this. Be happy. You made it. You did this."

I shook my head. "No. Nan would never give me blood. She hates me," I explained, and my throat burned, causing me to choke.

"Give her some water," he instructed the nurse.

"Small sips," she said as she held the cup to my mouth.

I did as instructed and winced as it burned my raw throat.

"Your throat will be raw for a day or so. You've had a feeding tube in for days. We just removed it after you woke up the first time," the nurse explained.

"Now, about being awake. You think you're still asleep because your sister gave you blood when you needed it?" the doctor asked.

I nodded.

"I assure you that you're awake. Sometimes people change when faced with situations that are life-threatening. You and your sister may not get along, but she didn't want you to die. She was willing to help."

I managed to stop crying and let him check me out.

When he opened the door and told me he would see about getting me moved to a normal room, my father came barreling in, looking like Kiro the Rock Star Manning.

"My baby girl doesn't do normal. I want the best. The *motherfucking best*. You got that? She needs room to rest and get better," Kiro barked at the doctor.

The doctor raised his eyebrows at me and then nodded his head before stepping out of the room. Normally, I would be embarrassed, but I was just so happy to see him. That I was alive to see him.

"Hey, Daddy," I said, and he was at my side immediately.

"I knocked out Mase to get here first. I couldn't wait. His momma may clock me when I get back out there, but I'm not scared of Maryann. I had to see you. Scared the shit outta me, girl. I fucking don't have that many years left, and you just shaved off at least ten of them. I think I died a thousand deaths from the moment I got that call about you. Damn near killed Grant Carter," he said as he gently rubbed my head.

My wild, insane, passionate daddy. "I love you," I told him.

His face crumpled, and he bent down to kiss my cheek. "I love you, too, baby girl."

"I have a baby girl now," I told him. "Have you seen her?"

A pained look crossed his face, and he shook his head. "I haven't. I couldn't. I just couldn't, Harlow. I thought I'd lost you."

I was his baby. Not Lila Kate. I understood that. "Grant said she's perfect," I told him.

"She's yours, baby. I don't see how she could be anything less than perfect."

I squeezed his hand and ran my finger over my initials tattooed on his knuckles, along with my mother's. He had gotten them done the day after I was born. He loved to tell me the story about how he had been so happy about his girls that he had to brand us on his body. "They said that Nan gave me blood," I said, watching his face.

He frowned, and I could tell this confused him, too. "Yeah,

she did. Can't figure it out. None of us could, but then, Rush was guarding her like a damn watchdog, so I ain't talked to her. But she did you a solid. Might be something that isn't completely twisted and evil underneath all that after all."

I smiled. I really hoped there was.

Grant

I opened the door to Lila Kate's room and found Blaire sitting in the rocker, humming a song. Her eyes found me, and she nodded toward the incubator.

"They made me put her back about thirty minutes ago. They had to change her and check her and feed her. I've been sitting here with her, humming to help her fall asleep."

"Harlow's awake. She's talking," I said, still loving how good that sounded. Blaire shot up out of the rocking chair and threw herself into my arms. The happy cry she let out made me laugh.

"She's awake! Oh, thank God! She's awake! She's gonna be OK, Grant!" She wiped at her tears. "All those letters . . . I didn't read them, but I knew what they were, and I sat in Lila Kate's room and cried like a baby. It broke my heart that she had even thought she needed to do that. But she's OK. She won't have to share herself with her baby girl through letters."

"Kiro's with her now. He actually shoved Mase down and ran past him to get to her first when I went to tell them. I was going to see what I could do about getting Lila Kate to Harlow. She wants to see our baby girl."

Blaire was still sniffing and wiping at her face. "She needs to see her. Go talk to them. I can stay in here with her if you want me to."

"No. Nate's in the waiting room with Rush. Go see your son. You've been here with me since this happened. You and Rush go home and get some rest."

Blaire smiled and nodded. "OK. But I'm only taking a bath and a quick nap, then I'll be back to see Harlow. I'm ready to plan this wedding."

"Thanks, Blaire. Thanks for being her friend. She's never had anyone like you. Thanks for loving her."

Blaire put her hands on her hips. "Stop making me cry, Grant Carter," she said.

"Sorry. But I mean it."

Blaire sighed and sniffed again. "I know you do. That's why I'm on the verge of tears again."

"Go find your family, and y'all go on home and rest. I'll call when she's ready for visitors."

Blaire nodded and hugged me again before leaving the room.

I walked over to the incubator and stared down at our Lila Kate. I never knew I wanted a baby. Not something I had ever thought about before Harlow. But now that I had her, I couldn't imagine life without her.

"She's awake. Your mommy is awake, and she's waiting for you. She woke up for us, and we have a lifetime of memories to start making."

❖

An hour later, we had Lila Kate in a rolling bed, and we were heading down to Harlow's room. Since Lila Kate's lungs were fully developed and she had shown no signs of any problems, they felt it was safe to let her spend some time with her mother. Today was the first day she had really started eating properly. Harlow was going to get to feed her. They were bringing the bottle down with her.

I opened the door and checked to make sure Harlow was awake and that Kiro and Mase had left. Harlow was sitting up and sipping water. She was alone except for a nurse. I couldn't wait to see her smile when I rolled in our daughter.

"I have someone really important waiting to meet you. She's been as patient as can be expected, but she's ready now," I said. I held the door as the nurse rolled Lila Kate into the room.

Harlow's eyes went wide with wonder as she gazed at our baby girl. Lila Kate had slept through the ride down here, so she was still unaware of this moment and how important it was.

"Can I hold her? Will it hurt her? I want to hold her, but I don't want to hurt her," Harlow said, her voice still weak.

The nurse adjusted pillows on each side of Harlow. "The best thing for her right now is to be in her mother's arms. She will have missed your voice and your heartbeat. She's been waiting for this, I can assure you."

Harlow's eyes were on our daughter, and mine were on her. The nurse picked up Lila Kate and placed her securely in Harlow's arms. I stood as close to them as I could while taking in the sight I had been afraid I would never see.

"She's beautiful," Harlow breathed, with a worshipful look on her face.

"Told you," I reminded her.

"She's so small. Is it OK that she's so small?" she asked, looking from me to the nurse.

"She was born two months early. She's four pounds, which is a really good weight for a thirty-two-week preemie. Her lungs are great, and so is her heart. She's even taking the bottle with no problem."

Harlow touched her little hands and ran her finger over her delicate nose as she studied her. "I get to watch her grow up," Harlow whispered. "I get to be her mother."

"The world's best mother," I said, watching my girls together for the first time.

Harlow spent the next few minutes checking out Lila Kate's toes and fingers and even her tummy. She checked everything. While I was helping her put socks on Lila Kate's little feet, the baby's little eyes fluttered open, and she puckered up.

"Hey, my precious baby, it's Mommy. I'm here," Harlow said. The puckered frown disappeared instantly, and Lila Kate gazed up at Harlow.

I grabbed my phone out of my pocket and snapped a photo of that moment. They were lost in each other's eyes, and I wasn't sure who was more in love with whom. It was one of those moments that there are no words to adequately capture. Nothing was good enough.

Lila Kate stuck her tiny thumb into her mouth and continued looking at her mother.

Harlow glanced up at me and beamed. "She's sucking her thumb." The awe in her voice was something I completely understood.

"She's been doing it since the first day. She also likes to add a finger in there every once in a while."

Harlow laughed, and Lila Kate stopped sucking. Her little

eyes went wide with wonder, as if she was just realizing who was holding her.

"You're our beginning," Harlow told her. "It's time we lived without fear. You're the most wonderful chance I ever took."

I bent over and kissed Harlow's forehead. "Thank you for her," I said. Then I lowered my head and kissed the other love of my life on the head.

Harlow

The day after I woke up, I was moved to a large suite. That was the best way to describe it. This room wasn't covered by health insurance and was hardly ever used, but it was on Kiro's bill, and it was the best they had to offer. I was thankful for it. The extra bed for Grant and the large sofa and extra seating for guests were nice. It didn't feel so cramped. If I was going to be stuck in a hospital, then this was a nice way to experience it.

Grant walked into the room carrying my overnight bag which Blaire had been holding on to for me. "They said they would give you a shower today, and I wanted you to have your bodywash and nightgown," he said.

"Thank you."

He set the bag down beside the bed and kissed me on the mouth sweetly before stepping back. "Maryann wants to see you. She's been wanting to visit with you before she heads back to Texas."

Mase had said his mother had come in with him to see me when I wasn't awake. She'd left to rest just before I had called out for Grant, and then everything had happened after that. I wanted to see her and thank her for being the first person to stand by me when I chose to keep my baby. "Good. I want to see her," I said.

Grant pointed to the large bouquet of pink roses and the wrapped gift beside it. "That's from her. She brought it last night, and I had them send it up here."

I turned to study the roses more closely while I waited for Maryann to arrive. When the door opened back up, I smiled at her, and she burst into tears. Her big, wide, happy smile was the only thing that eased my mind. She was crying joyful tears. That I could handle.

"I had wanted you to have your baby, but when you didn't wake up . . ." She put her hand on her chest and let out a small gasp. "I blamed myself. I was so sure you were strong enough, and then, oh, I was . . . just don't do that again, OK?" she said as she wrapped her arms around me and hugged me tightly.

"Thank you for believing in me. She's the most wonderful, perfect, beautiful little girl in the world."

Maryann sighed and wiped at her face. "I knew she would be, but having your life hanging in the balance was something I hadn't been prepared for."

"I never would have forgiven myself if I hadn't kept her. I had to do it this way. It was the only choice. And now I get to be a mother. I get to be a Maryann and bake cookies with her and play ball in the yard with her. I get to do all those things you did with Mase. I had been so envious of him growing up, because he had you. Now I can be like you," I said honestly. Maryann was the person I most wanted to be.

"Gah, girl, you are making me a mess. I love you, sweetheart. You've always been special. You were the one thing that saved your father's soul. You and your mother. It takes a special person to reach that man, and you did it. You don't need to be like me—you will do a wonderful job being you."

I nodded, but I knew I would always want to give Lila Kate the things that Mase had as a child and that I had dreamed of.

"I'm heading back to Texas today. I'm taking Major with me before he does something stupid. I'm sure you'll see Mase for a few more days until he feels secure enough to leave you. He's an overprotective big brother of the best sort."

I couldn't agree more. "And I love him for it."

"I know you do," she said.

She started to leave, and I remembered the gift. "Thank you so much for the roses and the gift," I called out after her. She glanced back and grinned.

"You're welcome. The roses are for you. The gift is for Lila Kate."

I nodded, and Maryann left. Knowing she had dropped everything and lived in the waiting room while I fought to come back made my heart swell. She was truly the best woman I knew.

⊞

After another week in the hospital, I was allowed to go home under weekly doctor supervision and no strenuous activity. I was supposed to stay in bed most of the time. I even had a special diet, and my medication had been changed again.

Lila Kate had met all of her milestones in NICU. She would have been released to go home two days ago, but they allowed her to stay until I was released. The fact that Kiro had paid ridiculous amounts of money to make sure I had the best care must have had a little to do with their decision, I was sure. That and his celebrity status.

Grant stood at the door of my hospital room with Lila Kate tucked in his arms in the pink bonnet and gown I had bought for her all those months ago. I held her while he took our picture—I wanted it for her scrapbook. It would be another part of our story, just like all those letters were a part of our story. I had one I wanted to read to her tonight.

"You hold her, and I'll push the wheelchair. Your dad paid a moving service to pack up all these flowers, balloons, and gift baskets," Grant said as he pointed to the room full of tokens of everyone's wishes and congratulations. I didn't even realize I had this many people in my life who cared.

A white stuffed lamb caught my attention, and I turned to look up at Grant. "Get the lamb," I told him. He frowned and glanced back at the little lamb. It was made out of the softest cashmere and had a matching blanket. "The blanket, too," I added as he walked over to get it.

Nan hadn't been by to see me or Lila Kate. Mase had mentioned that she had left after the announcement that I was awake and hadn't returned. I figured that she had originally come here for selfish reasons, although I was grateful, whatever her reason was. She had come through for me. Then, two days ago, a gift had arrived—a French layette that I had seen while surfing the Web for baby clothing. The lamb and the blanket had been included. When I opened it, the card simply read: *Congratulations, Nan.*

That was it. Nothing else. But it had been something. She hadn't used it to gain Kiro's or anyone else's attention; she'd just sent a gift. It was so unexpected and special. Because no matter what happened in the future, I would never forget what she did for me.

"Isn't this the gift Nan sent?" Grant asked as he tucked it in beside me.

"Yes, it is," I replied. I didn't explain myself further.

He nodded and pushed me with Lila Kate down the long hall, to the elevator, then out to the hospital valet parking, where a silver Land Rover was parked.

"A gift from your father. He said you needed a family car now. Something safe," Grant explained as he walked over to open the door. "I tried to tell him I'd supply my family with a safe car, but he said it was his gift and that I didn't get a say. Add a few choice curse words in there, and you get the idea." Grant grinned as he walked back to me and scooped Lila Kate up into his arms like a pro.

"You've got some pretty luxurious travel digs, too. Compliments of Gramps," Grant told her as he buckled her into her car seat, which looked very complicated. Grant seemed to know what he was doing.

When he finished, he took my hand, gently led me out of the wheelchair, and walked me over to the passenger door. "How did you know how to buckle her in?" I asked as I got in.

"I've been studying the manual for the past three days. When Kiro brought it with the Land Rover, I figured I'd better make sure I was using it correctly."

He was *that* dad. The one I had wanted so much for him to be. He adored our little girl, and he was reading safety manuals for car seats.

"You're wonderful," I told him, and he smirked.

"You just now figuring that out?"

He closed my door and went around the car to get in on the driver's side. Instead of starting the car, he stared a moment, then turned to look at me. He went pale.

"What's wrong?" I sat up straight and leaned over to touch his leg. Was he going to be sick?

"I have to drive her. I didn't . . . I guess I didn't think about that until this moment. She's so tiny."

I bit back a smile, because he was very serious. "Grant, drive us home. Now. You are a safe driver, and she is in a safe vehicle and a top-of-the-line car seat. You can do this, baby. You're overthinking it."

He nodded and took a deep breath, then started up the car. We pulled out slowly, made our way out of the parking lot, and headed home.

Grant went ahead of us and turned on her bedroom light. I waited outside the door, holding an alert and happy Lila Kate. She had woken up happy when we got her out of her car seat. She didn't like being strapped down and seemed thrilled to be getting out of it.

"Welcome home," I told her as we stepped into her room. I held her so she could see every part of her room. The huge unicorn that Dean Finlay had sent stood in the corner, and her little eyes kept going back to its bright colors. Grant motioned for me to sit in the glider.

"You need to rest. You can hold her, but sit while you're doing it."

He was back to taking care of me, and I knew after what he had been through, I had to let him. For a man who was scared of loving someone and losing them, he had grabbed on with both hands and held on tight. He hadn't allowed me to give up. When I'd been trying so hard to open my eyes in the hospital room, I'd heard his voice. *I don't accept that I won't get forever with you.*

I hadn't accepted it, either. At that moment, I had known I'd open my eyes. He had needed me to, and I had been ready to see our baby girl.

My sweet Lila Kate,

Today we brought you home from the hospital. I've been wrapped up in your beautiful face for the past week. I wasn't there right away for you. It was just you and Daddy for the first two and a half days. But I came back. I opened my eyes. I missed your daddy, and I couldn't wait to meet you.

We have so many things to experience together. I look forward to the day you say your first word and the day you take your first steps. I imagine your daddy and I will be a mess when we take you to your first day of kindergarten. When you tell me about your first crush. When I roll your hair for your first dance. When I see you in your cap and gown as you graduate from high school and go on to achieve great things.

But right now, I want to hold you and kiss each of your little toes. I want to read you the books I filled your room with. I look forward to our sleepless nights together and the times you spit up all over me and I have to change. Those little things won't be a chore or difficult for me. I will embrace them, because I almost didn't get to experience them at all.

So you take your time growing up. I don't want to rush a thing. I want to savor every moment. The good, the

*messy, and the messier. Bring it on, Lila Kate, because I
look forward to every minute of it.*

Love you always,
Mommy

Grant

Harlow was bathing, and I was on Lila Kate duty. She was sleeping peacefully, but Harlow didn't like for her to wake up and cry because we weren't there. Harlow said she was scared, and she wanted to make sure we were there.

I laid the stack of letters wrapped in the red satin ribbon down in front of me on the bed. I was almost afraid to look at the descriptions on each one. I didn't want to think about the circumstances in which I would have to read these. It hurt even to think about. But Harlow had written these letters for me.

One was labeled for the day after her funeral. One was for the first time I took care of Lila Kate alone. One was for the day she started kindergarten. One was for the day I thought I could love again. That one I wasn't going to be able to open, because that day would have never come. I couldn't love someone else or even try to, because it wouldn't have been fair to that person. In my heart, it would have always been Harlow. No one could take her place. And every time our daughter smiled up at me, I would be able to see her mother and remember the sacrifice she made so this perfect little girl could have a life.

"You're being quiet. Are you asleep?" Harlow called out from her bath.

I picked up the letters and walked to the bathroom. She noticed them immediately, and a smile touched her lips. If I didn't have her, these letters would have been golden. But she was here.

"Are you going to read them?" she asked.

I looked down at them and then back at her. "No," I replied. "I don't need to. They were for a Grant who didn't have his Harlow. I have my Harlow. That Grant doesn't exist. The broken, empty man you wrote these to will never exist. But I'm going to keep them. Pack them away. Maybe one day, we'll pull them down and remember. Just not today."

She tilted her head to the side, and a wet curl brushed her neck. "You wouldn't have been empty. Lila Kate would have filled the emptiness I left behind."

Maybe she would have. But she never could have made up for the fact that the women who owned my soul was gone. "Lila Kate will always be my baby girl. I will cherish and love her until the day I die. But you . . . you're the love of my life. You're my forever. I'll grow old loving you."

Harlow sighed, but it was a happy sigh. "You are a smooth talker, Grant Carter. A real smooth talker."

"Harlow?"

She sat up in the water. "Yes?"

"Will you marry me?"

She giggled and held up her ring finger, which had the diamond ring on it. "We already did this. Remember? I said yes."

"Tomorrow. Will you marry me tomorrow?"

She looked at me a moment like I had lost my mind. "We just got home from the hospital."

I nodded. "Yes, but I want to call you my wife. I want your last name to be Carter. I want you to be mine."

"I am yours. I have been for a very long time now."

"Please."

She bit her bottom lip and looked like she was contemplating it. Finally, she let her bottom lip free. "Three weeks. Give me three weeks. I can get Blaire's help to get a dress, and it will give your parents, my dad, and the Colts time to make plans to get back here. It doesn't have to be fancy. I actually prefer simple. But I want the people we love here."

I could give her three weeks if that was what she wanted. "Deal."

She stood up and pointed to the towels. "Could you hand me one of those? I need to call Blaire."

The bubbles and water running down her naked body commanded my complete attention. I couldn't touch her until her cardiologist cleared her. But looking at her was so damn nice.

"I'm getting cold." The laughter in her voice snapped me out of my lusting. I reached for a towel and walked over to her and wrapped it around her. Just as I was leaning in to kiss her, the cries of our daughter filled the room through the baby monitor.

Harlow gently shoved me. "Hurry, go check on her."

I turned and ran.

Stepping into her room, I turned on the light dimmer so the bright light didn't hurt her eyes. When she saw me standing over her, she stopped crying and kicked her feet and sucked hungrily on her fist. That was her hungry sign. The nurses had taught me that.

I picked her up and carried her over to the changing table to freshen her up, and then we went to see Mommy. I needed to go downstairs and fix a bottle, and Harlow wouldn't be OK with me leaving a fussing Lila Kate in her room.

"Someone's hungry and wants to visit with her mommy while I fix a bottle," I said, carrying Lila Kate over to her mother, who quickly slid her nightgown on and crawled up onto the bed so I could lay Lila Kate beside her.

"Hey, you," she cooed at our daughter. "You ready for something to eat? That hand won't taste good for long."

I left them upstairs and headed downstairs to get the bottle ready.

Harlow

I had been forced to shove Grant out the door this morning. He had been pacing and talking on the phone with a contractor. It had been forever since he'd worked, and he was spending a great deal of the time on the phone. The frustration etched on his forehead was hard to miss. Lila Kate was still sleeping a good portion of the day, and I rested when she did. When she was awake, we normally lay on my bed and talked and played. It wasn't difficult.

It was time for lunch, and she was getting fussy, so I brought her downstairs and laid her in the bassinet while I fixed her bottle. The doorbell rang just when I had her bottle warm enough. I pulled it out of the hot water and dried it off, then headed for the door.

A man I had never met before stood on the other side, but I didn't have to know him to figure out who it was. The similarities were too strong—his face was an older version of Grant's. This was his father. The man we never talked about.

Whenever I tried to mention him, the hurt look in Grant's eyes made me back off. I knew he had no idea where his mother was, and he said that when she called him, he'd let her know about the baby. I had gone through seven months of pregnancy, and two weeks had passed since Lila Kate's birth, and she still hadn't called to check in.

"Hello," I said, breaking the silence.

He smiled, and I could see he was nervous. Even his smile was like Grant's. "I'm, uh, I'm Brett Carter. Grant's dad."

I nodded. "I gathered that. The resemblance is uncanny," I said.

Brett chuckled. "No nonsense. Figured you'd be the type who won Grant over. He's had enough fake and flighty in his life."

I nodded, because I felt like he fell under the latter category. Or maybe he was just cold and insensitive. Grant had always wanted a relationship with this man—a real relationship—but he'd never gotten it.

"I just left the job site. He told me about the baby. Congratulations."

As if she knew we were discussing her, Lila Kate cried out, reminding me that she was hungry. "Thank you. It's lunchtime, and Lila Kate is hungry. You're welcome to come in and meet your granddaughter if you like."

I didn't wait for him to give me an excuse. I turned and left him standing there with the door wide open and went to get my fussing baby girl. She saw me holding the bottle and started kicking and fussing louder. She was ready for some food. I scooped her up and turned around to see that Brett had indeed followed me inside. He was staring at Lila Kate with concern.

"She's awfully small," he said.

"She was eight weeks early," I replied, cuddling her against me and giving her the bottle, which she greedily suckled. She closed her little eyes as if it was the best thing in the world. I knew for a fact that it was gross.

"Grant didn't tell me that. Did she have to stay in the hospital long?" he asked.

Was this guy for real? He didn't know anything? "Yes, she had to stay a little more than a week. So did I," I replied, then nodded toward the living room. "I need to sit down so she can be comfortable. We can take this in there."

He stepped back and let me pass.

I didn't check to see if he was following me. I headed for my large, comfy chair so I could cross my legs in front of me and let her lie in my lap while I fed her. She liked this position best, too.

I could see him taking a seat on the sofa across from us, and I waited until she was happily suckling again before I looked up at him.

"So you made it through OK, then," he said. I wanted to laugh. Where was he when his son was at the hospital thinking he was about to raise his daughter all by himself?

"Not exactly. I lost a lot of blood and blacked out, and then they had to put me under for emergency surgery. My heart stopped, but I was determined to live. A couple of days later, I woke up for good to a healthy baby girl and her terrified father."

Brett's eyes grew wide, and I could tell he hadn't been aware that things had been so bad. "I didn't realize. Grant left a message for me saying he was at the hospital with you and that you'd had the baby. He had told me to call him. I was busy, and I figured you two wanted time to spend with the baby and had enough visitors as it was, so I went to see him at the job site today. He wasn't very informative. He barely looked at me." He let out a sigh. "I guess I can understand why now. I just . . . when he said to call him, I didn't think I had to right then. I figured it was about work, and I knew I would need to pick up his slack while he was with you and the baby."

That was no excuse. His son had said he was at the hospital and his child had been born and asked his father to call him. He should have called. His job wasn't more important than his son. And he had a pretty damn fantastic son. "Grant's a wonderful man. A great man. The kind of man anyone would be proud to call theirs. I'll be proud to call him my husband, and I know Lila Kate already adores him. She follows the sound of his voice when he's in a room. She'll never have a moment in her life when she won't be proud of her father. Men don't get any better than Grant. He's the best. And I recognize that. I cherish it and honor it.

"But you don't realize the gift you have. He wants a real relationship with you. I can see the hurt in his eyes when your name comes up. My crazy, wild, rock-star father was there at the hospital with us. He isn't perfect, but he cared. He was there. He had to deal with fans and media while he was there, but he was there. You couldn't even call your son back and ask if he was OK. If his baby was OK. I don't understand you, Mr. Carter."

I decided to stop. I could scold this man and tell him how awful he was all day long, but I had said all that needed to be said.

Brett Carter stood up and stuck his hands into his pockets. He was leaving. Well, good riddance. He hadn't even stuck around to hold his granddaughter. I wondered if she would ever know this man. Or would her only grandparent be the one and only Kiro Manning?

"You're right. About all of it," he said as he started for the door. He stopped just outside the arched doorway. "I'm glad he found you. You're worthy of him. He's a lucky man."

Then he left.

Nan

I held the invitation in my hand as I stood at the edge of the water and let the waves crash and wash over my feet. If I stood here long enough, my feet would sink in the sand to my ankles. It was an odd habit, but I did this almost every day, except in the winter when the water was just too cold.

Today I had come out here to think. I'd expected the invitation to arrive. It was happening. That much I had known even before I heard that Grant had knocked up Harlow. But seeing it was different. It was more final.

Once I had thought that Grant Carter was the one man who would see me. The me underneath. The me I was scared to show the world. The me who had been so emotionally bruised because I'd worn my heart on my sleeve as a kid. When I got older, I put that me on lockdown so tightly it made it impossible for people to hurt me.

But it made it easy for them to hate me.

There were very few people who didn't just use me. My brother was Rush Finlay, son of the famous drummer Dean Finlay. For years, my so-called friends just wanted to get near my brother. They wanted an in. And I let them have it, because watching him screw them and throw them away was what they deserved. It was my way of taking revenge.

Then I had found out Rush wasn't the only one with a celebrity father. Kiro Manning had been my dad all along. Yet he had never claimed me or tried to have any relationship with me. That had almost cracked me and the steel walls around my heart. His refusal to acknowledge me had almost made me completely lose my mind. Rush had been there, though, and he'd loved me. He had always been the one to love me. When no one else did, my big brother accepted me no matter how awful I acted. He didn't approve, but he saw the me underneath.

Then Blaire had taken him from me. She'd won his heart and given him a son, and now he had little room for his messed-up sister. I hated Blaire for that. I hated that she took him away. I wanted to hate their kid, too, but damned if Nate wasn't the cutest kid in the world. I couldn't hate him. It was impossible.

Grant Carter had stepped in and been there when I needed someone to care. Rush was busy with his new family, and Grant had taken over his role with a different twist. Grant wasn't my brother, and he was gorgeous. So we started screwing around, too—a friends-with-benefits thing. He didn't expect me to be nice, and I didn't expect him to just fuck me. He was so sweet at times, and he made things better when no one else could. Or even wanted to. He knew how to make me laugh.

But just like any good thing that comes my way, I pushed him away because I had let him get too close. I refused to accept that maybe he could love me. I was terrified to open myself up to rejection yet again.

While I was pushing Grant away, his head was turned by the complete opposite of me. A girl who had the love of her father. She was quiet and unassuming. She wasn't mean to anyone. Ever. She was matter-of-fact but soft-spoken. She was the perfect person for Grant. I was not. I was the fucked-up brat who didn't feel secure enough to let herself get close to someone.

Grant fell in love with that girl, and it happened right under my nose. While I was screaming and cursing, she was quiet and calm. It would have taken an idiot not to choose her. She was the easy one to love. I was impossible.

I looked down at the invitation again. Harlow Manning had never done anything to me other than have the love of a father we shared. It wasn't her fault. She didn't beg for it or demand it—she just had it. I could blame her, but it would be pointless. From what I had seen, her life hadn't been peaches just because Kiro Manning loved her. He still sucked balls at being a father. But then, having a rock star for a parent was never a positive thing.

I had been unfair to her . . . no, I had been cruel to her. But I had paid my dues. I made up for my wrongs with her. Now I could walk away and let Grant and Harlow Carter live their happily ever after. They had a baby girl and a house with a white picket fence. That was what they both deserved.

I didn't deserve shit. I was alone in this world, and it was all my fault. I didn't see that ever changing, because I would have to let the me I once was free, and I couldn't do that again. Any more rejection, and I wasn't sure I'd make it. Finding a reason to live was becoming more and more difficult.

This was my life. And I'd created it.

Grant

Harlow hadn't even flinched when I'd said we didn't need to send my dad an invitation to the wedding. He'd never mentioned his visit to our house, but Harlow had told me every detail. If he didn't want to say anything to me about my baby girl, then he didn't deserve to be a part of my wedding.

However, I had flinched when she'd said she wanted to invite Nan. Harlow's whole attitude toward Nan had changed ever since she found out about Nan giving her blood. Although Nan was already back to her normal nasty self, as far as I could tell. I had seen her at the club bitching at Rush about something. Her haughty glares were also firmly in place. She hadn't even acknowledged Blaire when she'd walked up to Rush. Didn't seem to matter with Harlow, though. She would never forget what Nan had done. It was hard for me to forget, too. If she wanted to invite Nan and try to reach out to her, then I was more than willing to let her. However, all bets were off the moment Nan did anything that upset Harlow. I had my limits.

The rest of the invitations were sent out to everyone we loved and cared about in our lives. Lila Kate had lain in a blanket on the floor while we sat down at the table beside her and addressed all the envelopes. She had been happy to listen to us talk. It was moments like these that made me get choked up. The idea that I almost didn't have this got to me if I dwelled on it too much.

The girls had been getting ready upstairs while I had break-fast. I heard Harlow talking to Lila Kate as she walked down the stairs, and I set down my cup of coffee and went to meet them. Harlow was dressed in jeans and a long-sleeved shirt, since the fall was finally starting to show up. It was normally warm here until November, but we were getting a few cooler days already.

Lila Kate had a whole new wardrobe now, thanks to Blaire. She had come over with preemie clothing, because nothing but the baby gowns fit her, and even those were big. Harlow didn't want to leave the house yet, so Blaire had brought the clothes to her. They had gone through what looked like hun-dreds of outfits before settling on the ones that Harlow liked best. Today she had dressed her in a onesie covered in lots of yellow butterflies.

"Look who's waiting for you," Harlow said as she reached the bottom step. "Daddy's here."

"I was actually waiting for both of you," I told her, and kissed her lips. "You look good enough to eat this morning."

Harlow giggled. "That can be arranged."

"Mommy's being naughty. I like it," I teased her. Her beau-tiful smile grew bigger.

I took Lila Kate from her arms and placed her against my chest. I held her head as she reared back to try to look up at me. "You have fun dress shopping today. Buy whatever the hell you want."

She was going shopping for a wedding dress with Blaire and Della. Della was also looking for a dress. Her wedding was several months away, but they were doing a joint shopping trip and making a girls' day out of it. Blaire had invited Bethy, but she had used the excuse that she needed to work some extra hours. Blaire was worried about her, which made all of us worried about her. She was pulling away more and more. Someone had to reach her, I just didn't know who could do it. I did know Jace wouldn't have wanted this. He wouldn't have wanted her to grieve for this long.

"You two have fun while I'm gone. I'm nervous about leaving, but not because I don't think you can handle it. I just haven't been away from her since I woke up. I don't like the idea of not being able to see her whenever I want to." We had been home a little more than a week now, and Harlow hadn't left the house. The doctor recommended that we keep Lila Kate at home for the first month while her little body and immune system matured some more. While I had gone to work, Harlow had stayed here happily. Blaire almost had to plead to get her to look for a wedding dress.

"I'll have my phone in my pocket. Every time you want to see her, just FaceTime me. Now, go have fun," I said, swatting her on the ass and nodding my head toward the door.

She grinned and rolled her eyes at me. "Fine. I'll go," she agreed, but then leaned in to kiss Lila Kate's head one more time. "I'll be back soon," she said.

Lila Kate got so excited by Harlow that she buried her face in my chest. I kept my hand at the back of her neck, because she'd throw it back again to see if Harlow was still nearby any second now.

"She looks more like you now," Harlow said, touching her little arm.

"She's too pretty to look like me," I replied.

Harlow cocked an eyebrow at me. "I know you don't like hearing this, but you're pretty, too, pretty boy."

Chuckling, I opened the door and kissed her lips one more time just as Blaire's Mercedes SUV pulled into our driveway. Harlow waved good-bye and blew us kisses, then finally left the house for the first time.

I watched until she was safely in Blaire's car and was pulling away until I closed the door. "Want to bet your mommy calls us in the next ten minutes?" I asked Lila Kate as we walked to the kitchen to get her a bottle and finish my coffee. "She won't be able to help herself. Being away from you isn't something she's fond of. But I need her to get that dress so I can marry her. Then we'll be official. The Carter family. Has a nice ring to it, doesn't it?"

To the woman who gave me everything,

Today's the day I get to give you my name. It doesn't seem like enough, but then, you've had my heart and soul now for more than a year. This is all I have left to give you. What you've given me is so much more.

I decided, since Lila Kate and I had so many letters from you, that it was time you got a letter, too. You deserve a letter more than anyone else. You are, after all, the hero of our story. Without you and your determination, we wouldn't all be standing in front of family and friends today with our little girl in our arms, pledging forever to each other. As if we needed a ceremony for that.

You became my forever even before I realized it.

Thank you for being brave. Braver than anyone I know. Thank you for showing me that when we want something badly enough, it's worth taking all the risks and chances to get even a taste.

When I thought I had lost you, not once did I regret letting myself love you. I was shattered, but in my heart, I was so damn thankful for those memories. For letting myself have that time with you. I found out that life is about experiencing those moments when you're so happy you feel like your chest will burst. We need those cherished memories to hold on to during those moments when the world comes crashing down.

I didn't understand that until I was there. While you were asleep, all I could do was remember the good times. The sound of your laughter and how incredible you felt in my arms. How being with you made everything right. It's what got me through. It's what helped me hold our baby girl for the first time alone, not knowing if you'd ever see her face.

Thank you for loving me. I'm the luckiest man in the world. I know a lot of men claim that, but they have no idea. They don't have you. And they haven't held my baby girl. I have it all, and I couldn't ask for more.

With love from your adoring, lucky-as-hell husband,
Grant

Harlow

I folded the letter and wiped away the tears that were now running down my face. Crazy man had to make me cry before I walked down the aisle. I used the tissue in my hand to blot away the wetness and took a deep breath. I would probably need to frame this, because I was going to read it so often the paper was going to wear through.

"Why are you crying?" Blaire asked as she stepped into the room.

I held up the letter. "This. It's from Grant," I explained. "I don't think it was supposed to make me cry, but it did."

"Ah, I understand. Rush had me in a fit of tears before I walked down the aisle."

Smiling, I remembered their wedding. It had been beautiful and much more elaborate than this one would be. I had wanted simple, and Grant had agreed.

"We have a five-minute drive. You ready to go?" she asked me.

"Yes. Is Lila Kate ready?"

She nodded. "Yep. She looks like an angel. Her mommy might not be wearing white, but she's rocking her own fluffy white gown."

Laughing, I slipped on my flats and tucked the letter into my jewelry box. "Let's do this," I said, heading out my bedroom door and toward Lila Kate's room. She was lying in her crib, looking at her slipper-covered feet in fascination. When her gaze found mine, she kicked happily. "We have a handsome prince waiting for us. We need to go." I scooped her up.

She did look adorable in her dress.

Blaire led us out to my Land Rover, and I buckled Lila Kate in before climbing into the passenger seat. My dress was easy. I hadn't gone for the long, white, traditional wedding dress. Instead, my dress was the palest of blues. It reminded me of the color of the sky when looking through a cloud. It was a simple yet elegant satin gown that belted at the waistline and flowed outward, falling just above my knees.

Lila Kate gurgled and let us know she was back there with a little fussing. We turned toward the club, then drove back to the private beach for homeowners only. Woods had offered to let us use the stretch of beach in front of his house. We wouldn't have any uninvited spectators, and it would be private.

Blaire pulled up to the rose-covered archway that served as the entrance to the wedding. "This is your stop," she said, grinning. "Nervous?"

I shook my head. "No. Not at all. I've never been more ready to do anything in my life."

After stepping out of the car, I quickly scooped Lila Kate out of her car seat before she got too frustrated and tucked her in my arms. She was still less than six pounds, but she was gaining weight steadily, and that was what mattered.

"Let's go see Daddy," I whispered. We stepped up to the archway. Blaire straightened her dress and quickly sent a text to let them know we were ready, since we couldn't be seen on this side of the house.

The music started up, and Blaire wiggled her fingers in a wave before picking up a small bouquet of three roses—a pink one centered between two white ones. It was a symbol of our family. I would have carried it myself, but I had my hands full of something much more important.

Blaire walked away down the aisle, and I counted to twenty just like we had practiced, before Lila Kate and I made our way down the rose-petal-covered walkway. We made the turn around the house, and there they were, all standing up and turning toward us. The people we loved. I smiled as Lila Kate's gaze took everything in.

It wasn't until we were at the center looking straight up the aisle that I saw him. Our handsome prince. His eyes locked on mine.

He thought I was the hero of our story. How wrong he was. He had been the hero all along.

Acknowledgments

Writing this second half of Grant and Harlow's story was a journey for me I didn't expect when I started. I've never cried so much while writing, editing, and rereading a book in my life. I've always loved Grant. I am so pleased that his story turned out the way it did. He was special, and his story deserved to be just as special.

First of all, I want to thank the Atria team. The brilliant Jhanteigh Kupihea. I couldn't ask for a better editor. She is always positive and working to make my books the best they can be. Thank you, Jhanteigh, for being awesome. Ariele Fredman and Valerie Vennix for being not only brilliant with your ideas but listening to mine. Judith Curr for giving me and my books a chance. And everyone else at Atria that had a hand in getting this book to production. I heart you big-time.

My agent, Jane Dystel. She is always there to help in any situation. I'm thankful that I have her on my side in this new and ever-changing world of publishing. Lauren Abramo, who handles my foreign rights. I couldn't begin to think of conquering that world without her.

The friends who listen to me and understand me the way no one else in my life can: Colleen Hoover, Jamie McGuire, and Tammara Webber. You three have listened to me and supported me more than anyone I know. Thanks for everything.

My beta readers, Natasha Tomic and Autumn Hull. You both are brilliant and know exactly where to point out what is missing. Thank you so much for keeping up with my hectic schedule. Beta reading for someone who is always writing a book isn't an easy job.

Last by certainly not least:

My family. Without their support I wouldn't be here. My husband, Keith, makes sure I have my coffee and the kids are all taken care of when I need to lock myself away and meet a deadline. My three kids are so understanding, although once I walk out of that writing cave they expect my full attention, and they get it. My parents, who have supported me all along. Even when I decided to write steamier stuff. My friends, who don't hate me because I can't spend time with them for weeks at a time because my writing is taking over. They are my ultimate support group, and I love them dearly.

My readers. I never expected to have so many of you. Thank you for reading my books. For loving them and telling others about them. Without you I wouldn't be here. It's that simple.

Read on for a look at the next Rosemary Beach novel,
which finally reveals the story of Tripp and Bethy

You Were Mine

Available from Atria Books in eBook and
trade paperback in December 2014

Prologue
Tripp

Everyone has that defining moment in their life. That one choice you have to make. I had my moment, and it has haunted me ever since. In those defining moments, you either pave a road to happiness or you regret every step from then on. For me, I don't know which road would have been the best, because between my two choices, neither of them included *her*.

I had been young and so fucking scared. Scared of being forced by my parents to be someone I didn't want to be. Scared of making the wrong choice. Scared of leaving her. But mostly I'd been scared of losing her.

She was my greatest regret. Leaving her changed me. The moment I climbed on my bike and drove out of Rosemary Beach, Florida, I left true joy behind. I'd only had that summer with her, three months that altered me forever. But what I would never be able to forgive myself for was that they had changed her just as much. She was beyond broken now. I couldn't reach her.

Seeing her in pain broke my soul. Losing my cousin, Jace, had caused a deep pain in both of us, one I never wanted to relive. He would forever be in my heart. I'd never forget his laugh and the easy way he loved and lived his life. He didn't live in the world of fear I inhabited. He chose his path and he walked it. He was the better man. And I had been able to stand back and let him have her. She deserved the better man.

Now he was gone, and both our worlds were thrown off balance. Because I couldn't stand back anymore. No one was protecting her. No one was holding her, but she wouldn't fucking let me near her. She wasn't going to let me fix the past. I'd severed any hope of that when I'd driven away and left her with no other choice but to be with Jace.

If only I could embrace the emptiness and accept it. But I couldn't. Not when I saw her lost, beautiful face. She needed me as much as I needed her. Our story wasn't over. It would never be over. If I had to stay here and watch over her, even though she wouldn't let me get near her, I would. For the rest of my motherfucking life. I'd stay right here. Making sure my Bethy was okay.

Tripp

Eight years ago . . .

It wasn't just another summer. It was my last summer here in Rosemary Beach. I was already feeling the suffocating presence of my father and his plans for me. He was so sure I'd leave for Yale in the fall. I'd gotten in, thanks to his connections. He'd made me take a tour of the campus, and once I was in, he'd forced me to accept. *Nobody turns down Yale.* It was all that ever came out of his mouth anymore. Yale this, Yale that. Goddamn Yale.

I wanted to be on my Harley. I wanted another fucking tattoo. I wanted to feel the wind in my hair and know I had nowhere I had to be. That life was free. I was free. Before this summer was over, I was going to ride off without a word. Leave behind the money and power that came with being a Newark and find my path. This wasn't my world. I would never fit in here.

"Hey, sweetie, I didn't see you walk in," London Winchester said as she slipped her arms around one of mine and held on. That was another reason I had to get the fuck out of here—London. My mother was already planning our wedding. Didn't matter that I'd broken up with her last month. London, her mother, and my mother all believed I was just going through a moody phase. My mother said it was okay if I needed to sow some wild oats this summer. London would be patient.

"Where's Rush?" I asked, glancing around the house full of people. If Rush Finlay was throwing parties again, then his mother and younger sister, Nan, had to be out of town. Rush owned the place. His father was the drummer in the legendary rock band Slacker Demon. His mother and sister benefited from all the money Rush got from his dad. Rush's mother had been a groupie once, and although Rush's dad, Dean Finlay, seemed to care about his kid, he didn't give a shit about Rush's mom. They never married. Nan had another father, who was out of the picture.

"Outside by the pool. Want me to take you to him?" she asked sweetly. That sweet tone was so fucking fake, it was ridiculous. The girl was venomous. I'd seen her in action.

"I can find him," I replied, shaking her loose and walking away without a backward glance.

"Really? This is how you're going to be now? I won't wait around on you forever, Tripp Newark!" she called out after me.

"Good," I said calmly over my shoulder, then headed into the crowd, hoping to get some people and distance between us. I'd been with her for two years. She'd been a really good fuck, and once I thought maybe she was it. But I could never actually say I was in love with her. This past year I realized I was simply tolerating her. I dreaded seeing her, and when I faced the facts, I realized I was keeping her around to make my parents happy. But I was done with that. No more keeping the parents happy. I was keeping me happy.

"Tripp!" Woods Kerrington called out from a circle of girls surrounding him. He was such a fucking Romeo. He made them all believe they had a chance. Holding in a chuckle, I nodded my head in his direction.

"What's up?"

"Hopefully, a lot of things real soon," he replied, and this time I laughed. "Jace is outside with Rush and Grant, if you're looking for him."

Jace was my younger cousin, and Woods was Jace's best friend. I'd had them both in my life for as long as I could remember.

"Thanks."

Turning through the crowd, I headed for the back door.

"Stop it! I said no, Jonathon. I'm not interested." I stopped in my tracks. That didn't sound good.

"I got you in here tonight and I'm not getting any thanks for it?" The guy was angry and sounded like a prick.

The girl didn't respond right away. I moved toward their voices and stopped outside of the kitchen. I recognized the Jonathon the girl was talking to. He was a tennis instructor at Kerrington Club, owned by Woods's family. He was also a notorious asshole and had fucked most of the cougars in town. If he was about to take advantage of this girl then I was going to throw his ass out.

"I just . . . I didn't know . . . I want to leave." The way the girl's timid voice cracked told me she was scared.

"Fuck that, bitch. I don't care how damn hot your tits are, I'm not dealing with this shit. You can find the door by yourself," Jonathon snarled.

I took a step toward the door as Jonathon stalked through it. Stupid little fuck.

I shoved him back into the kitchen three steps with one hard push. He was going to apologize for being a dickhead before I threw him out. I doubted Rush even knew he was here. Jonathon wasn't in our circle of friends. Some of the cougars he slept with included a couple of our mothers. Not on our favorites list.

Getting his sorry ass to apologize would do him some good. Poor girl should have known better than to mess around with the help at the club. Maybe she'd learn a lesson after this.

"What the fuck?!" he shouted, then his eyes widened when he realized who I was. My dad sat on the board at the Kerrington Club, and I could have Jonathon fired with one word. He knew it.

"That's what I was wondering, Jonathon. What the fuck? What the fuck are you doing at Finlay's house, and why the fuck are you treating your date so badly? She too young for you? I know you prefer the over-forty crowd," I said, taunting him. I wanted him gone. Just one wrong move, and that was all I needed to make sure he lost his job without feeling a shred of remorse.

"I didn't . . . . I mean, I was invited. I got an invite. This is just a girl whose aunt works at the club. She's not anybody."

Glancing over at the girl in question, I recognized her right away from her big brown eyes. She was Darla's niece, Bethy. I'd seen her before. Hell, it was hard to miss her. Jonathon was right about her tits. They were noticeable. But her sweet face and innocent look had kept me from moving in on that. Besides, Darla was scary as hell. She handled hiring the employees at the club, and she'd been there forever.

"Bethy, right?" I asked her.

Her big eyes got even bigger before she nodded.

"This guy's a douchebag, sweetheart. You shouldn't trust him. Be careful who you let take you out."

"You know her?" Jonathon asked incredulously, as if she were too beneath me to notice. Stupid shit was getting on my last nerve.

I turned my attention back to him. "Yeah. I know her aunt. The woman who hired your sorry ass. I wonder how she'd feel if she knew how poorly you were treating her niece."

Jonathon's fear was obvious. He had a good gig at the club, and he didn't want to lose it.

"Leave. Don't ever come back. Finlay finds out about this and he'll do more than give you a warning. He'll beat your sorry ass. He likes Darla. We all do. Stay the fuck away from her niece."

Jonathon turned his attention to Bethy. The furious gleam in his eyes was directed at her. She shrank further back, putting more distance between them until her back was pressed to the wall. Dickhead was getting off on scaring her. Stepping between the two of them, I glared at Jonathon. "Leave. Now."

I could tell it was taking everything he had to keep his mouth shut, but he did. I watched as he muttered a curse and turned to leave the kitchen. "Make sure you don't stop until you're off this property," I called out after him.

When he was gone, I turned back to Bethy. She was wringing her hands and looking nervous. I'd gotten rid of the prick. Why was she upset now?

"You good now?" I asked her.

She bit her bottom lip, then shrugged. "I, um, don't know."

She didn't know? I couldn't keep from grinning. She was pretty damn cute. But she was young. "Why don't you know?" I asked her. I enjoyed the way she talked. Her voice was husky but sweet.

She let out a small sigh and dropped her gaze to the floor. "He was my ride. I don't live close by."

As if I would let her get back in the car with that fucker. He had to be four years older than her. He was older than me.

"I'll give you a ride. I'm safe. Jonathon isn't. Besides, he's way too old for you. Dude would go to jail if he touched you."

She lifted her eyes back up to look at me. "I'm almost seventeen," she said, as if that were legal, though she was a little older than I expected.

She was so expressive. I liked that. She didn't try to bat her eyelashes or pucker her lips to look sexy. She was real. How long had it been since I'd been with a girl who was real? But then, she was young and she'd been raised in a very different world than I had.

"Yeah, sweetheart. But he's almost twenty. He shouldn't have gone anywhere near you."

She looked deflated, then nodded. Surely she hadn't wanted to stay with him? Fuck that, what was Darla teaching this girl?

"I'm sorry I ran him off, but he wasn't treating you right."

Those eyes went wide again, and a dimple appeared in her cheek. "Oh, don't apologize for that. He wanted me to go back to a bedroom and uh . . ." she trailed off. She didn't need to explain. I was pretty sure of what he wanted to do with her.

"Come on. Let's get you home," I said, nodding toward the door.